# The Alpha Plague 5

Michael Robertson

Website and Newsletter:
www.michaelrobertson.co.uk

Email: subscribers@michaelrobertson.co.uk

Edited by:
Aaron Sikes - www.ajsikes.com
Terri King - http://terri-king.wix.com/editing

Cover Design by Christian Bentulan

Formatting by Polgarus Studio

The Alpha Plague 5
Michael Robertson
© 2017 Michael Robertson

*The Alpha Plague 5* is a work of fiction. The characters, incidents, situations, and all dialogue are entirely a product of the author's imagination, or are used fictitiously and are not in any way representative of real people, places or things.

Any resemblance to persons living or dead is entirely coincidental.

All rights reserved

No part of this publication may be reproduced, stored in a retrieval system or transmitted in any form or by any means electronic, mechanical, photocopying, recording or otherwise, without the prior written permission of the author except in the case of brief quotations embodied in critical articles and reviews.

Would you like to be notified when I have a new release?
Join my mailing list for all of my updates here:-

www.michaelrobertson.co.uk

# Chapter One

No matter how Vicky shifted on the hard blue floor, she couldn't get comfortable. She'd even stood up and paced up and down outside Flynn's cell, but nothing helped.

It hadn't been the first time she'd done it, but Vicky looked at all of the other rooms that lined the corridor with Flynn's cell on it. Many of them had locked doors; a few holding cells had vertical bars that ran across a small square hole resembling a window. They'd put Flynn in the cell without one—Hugh had said they didn't have a clean cell with a window in it. Vicky peered into the darkness of each of the ones with the barred holes, and although her heart raced to stare into the shadows in case anything jumped up, they not only all seemed empty, but they all seemed clean too.

A deep breath and Vicky inhaled the reek of bleach in the corridor. Home stank of the stuff and rightly so, but maybe this was a little bit excessive. Maybe—as a clean freak—Hugh had been bothered by the fact that the cells hadn't been bleached yet. Maybe that would be enough for him to force Flynn into a room where Vicky couldn't see him. Or maybe Hugh had another agenda.

When Vicky and Rhys had gone out scavenging in Biggin Hill, some days they only found cleaning products. There hadn't been much need for cleanliness at the shipping containers, but in a place like Home, a virus could tear through it like wildfire. So many bodies in an enclosed space seemed like a breeding ground for an epidemic. The reek of cleanliness might have been borderline offensive, but better to be safe. Something about Hugh just didn't sit right though; there seemed to be an overly strong element of control in his need to keep everything spick and span.

Vicky stood up and shook the inaction from her body as she wiggled her legs. She then knocked on the white wooden door of Flynn's cell and called, "Flynn?"

The muffled reply of the boy came back at her. "Yep."

"Does it smell of bleach in your cell?"

"Huh?"

Maybe he hadn't heard her properly through the door. Maybe he had and thought he hadn't. Vicky repeated herself anyway. "Does it smell of bleach in your cell?"

A few more seconds of silence passed where Vicky pushed on the back of her kidneys and shoved her pelvis forward. It did little to ease the aching stagnation in her body. "Flynn?"

The boy had obviously chosen to ignore her question, because now she'd asked it again, his reply came back at her like the crack of a whip. "Why are you asking me about bleach?"

"It's just, I want to work out if it's clean—"

"Look, Vicky, I'm okay in this cell. I'm not going anywhere, so why don't you go and get some rest and come back in a day and a half when the quarantine period is up?"

"I left you once, Flynn, I won't do it again." Currently unable to see the boy's face, Vicky saw the memory of his dirty hand as the earth consumed him in the tunnel. How the fuck had he gotten out of there? Had Jessica and Hugh not taken Flynn away so swiftly when he arrived at Home, then she would have asked him. It didn't seem right to ask him now from the other side of a locked door.

Vicky continued to talk to Flynn. The poor kid must have been going out of his mind in the cell on his own. "Although I lived with your family, I kept myself very separate—a different shipping container, a lot of time alone … At those crucial points when you probably needed someone to talk to, I wasn't there, emotionally at least. I saw all of this when I thought I'd lost you, and I want to make up for that. I want to be more connected to you and other people. Because of that, I'm not going anywhere. They seem like good people here at Home, but I don't want to leave your side, Flynn."

When Flynn didn't reply, Vicky sighed and sat back down on the hard and cold floor. Maybe he hadn't heard her. Maybe he'd decided the conversation would be too much effort and had chosen to reject it.

The *click* of boot heels snapped through the long corridor, and when Vicky looked around to see her approaching, both her heart and body sank.

The woman had a cushion in her hands as she strode toward Vicky with purpose.

When she got close—her features pulled back by her extreme blonde ponytail—Jessica handed the cushion to Vicky and revealed the tray of food she had in her other hand. "Here, you didn't look comfortable last time I saw you."

"I'm not," Vicky said as she looked down at the cream and pink pillow. "I'd be much more comfortable if you let him out and we both went to a room with a bed in it."

When Jessica glanced at Vicky, Vicky glared back. The two women held each other's stares before Jessica tilted her head to one side. "You know I can't do that."

"Well, let me in with him, then. If one of us turns, then at least we're both contained."

A tight smile that looked to be dragged back with her ponytail and Jessica shook her head. "Can't do that either."

"Is there anything you *can* do?"

Because Flynn hadn't been put in a room with a cell door, not only did it lack a barred window, but it also lacked a hatch to slide food through. With her eyes fixed on Vicky as if she would try to fight her way into the room, Jessica placed Flynn's tray of food on the floor, pulled a large ring of keys from her pocket, and unlocked Flynn's door with a loud and resounding *thunk*!

After she'd shoved his tray through with her toe, she closed the cell door again and locked it. All the while, she focused on Vicky.

The women stared at one another for a few more seconds before Jessica walked back the way she'd come from.

Once the *click* of Jessica's boots had vanished, Vicky leaned close to Flynn's door. "Hang on in there, mate."

Flynn didn't reply.

\*\*\*

It felt like days, but it could have only been four to five hours at the most by the time Hugh strode down the corridor toward Vicky. Having reluctantly accepted Jessica's gift of a cushion, Vicky's bottom appreciated the rest, if nothing else.

Like Jessica before him, Hugh carried a tray of food. The way he held onto either side of the tray highlighted his broad shoulders and prominent pecs. The boy's second meal now, Flynn had at least four or five more to go before they let him out.

Although less hostile than Jessica had been, Hugh watched Vicky all the same as he placed Flynn's tray of food on the floor and fished the keys from his pocket. As Jessica had done before him, he slid the tray of food in and locked the door again.

"That floor won't get any more comfortable, you know," he said to Vicky.

Vicky shuffled as if suddenly more uncomfortable because of Hugh's words. "There's a simple way to get me off this floor."

The smile told Vicky that Hugh wished he could do more. "Jessica's already told you the answer to that."

"Oh, has she now? Jessica been running back to you and relaying all of our conversations, has she?"

When Hugh crouched down, his combat trousers pulled tight, highlighting the man's power in his muscly legs. Clearly someone who exercised a lot, Hugh had the glow of a person in good physical health. He reached out and put a hand on her outstretched shin. "Look, Vicky, I understand you're frustrated, but we can't break the rules for you."

"But Flynn's only a kid."

"I'm not a kid, I'm sixteen," Flynn called through the locked door.

A tilt of his head toward Flynn's cell and Hugh smiled. "See, he's okay."

With her jaw in a tight clench, Vicky stared at Hugh and said nothing in response to his optimism.

As she watched Hugh walk away from them down the corridor, Vicky leaned close to Flynn's door. "I'm sorry, I didn't mean to call you a kid."

Again, Flynn didn't respond.

"I'm sorry, okay? I worry about you. A lot."

Flynn didn't reply to Vicky's comment; instead, he asked, "What are the plans for when I get out of here?"

"We're both going to rest and get our strength up. God knows we need it."

"And then?"

"And then, I dunno, we'll do our bit, I suppose. We're part of a community, so we'll need to pull our weight."

The silence of the corridor surrounded Vicky again as she pulled away from Flynn's door and leaned against the cold, hard white wall again.

\*\*\*

The wet pulse of the alarm sent Vicky's heart rate off the charts as she snapped awake. The bright glare from the strip lighting in the ceiling made it impossible to tell whether it was night or day.

The alarm continued to send a jagged sting into her eardrums as she blinked against the lights and found her bearings. A sharp pain speared the base of her neck from where she'd slept awkwardly.

It took Flynn banging on the other side of his cell door before Vicky heard him over the alarm. With her face pressed against the white wood, a slight sting on her cheek from the cold touch of it, she called through to him, "Are you okay?"

"Yep, what's that noise?"

"I don't know."

"Why don't you go and check it out?"

"Because I don't want to leave your side."

"I ain't going anywhere. What if it's a fire?"

The rubber sole sound of running shoes hit the hard floor and grabbed Vicky's attention. The noise came from the back of the complex. A second later, a man appeared at a flat out sprint and didn't even look at Vicky as he flew past her.

With her hands cupped around her mouth, Vicky called up the hallway after him, "Excuse me. What's that noise? Is there a problem?"

By the time she'd finished her questions, the man had vanished from sight.

The alarm continued to echo through the large complex. The loudness of it made her dizzy, so Vicky rested back against Flynn's door and called through to him again. "I think—" The alarm stopped and Vicky's loud voice echoed in the quiet corridor. She lowered the volume. "I think we're okay, mate. I don't think we have anything to worry about."

"How can you be sure?"

"I can't."

"And you don't want to check?"

"Remember I told you about the place I used to work in?"

"The Alpha Tower?" Flynn said.

"Yep. All of the white corridors and locked rooms here kind of remind me of that place—even that alarm sounds like theirs did. That's one of the most evil places I've ever been in, and while I don't think Home is anything like the Alpha Tower, I can't leave you here on your own. I'll wait until you come out, so please stop telling me to go away."

Muffled, like all of his other words, Flynn simply said, "Okay."

\*\*\*

No more alarms sounded and Vicky had tried to find comfort again on the solid floor. The thud of boots dragged her attention up the corridor and she saw Hugh walking toward her. It had been a good eight or nine hours since she'd seen him last. "What was that noise a few hours ago?"

With a bat of his hand, Hugh scoffed and said, "Just an alarm. Nothing to worry about."

"This ain't the kind of world you do fire drills in. I can't see all of the people in Home lining up outside as they take a register. Also, I saw a man tear down this corridor like his life depended on it."

A twinkle lit up Hugh's eyes and a hint of a smile lifted the edges of his mouth. "Flynn should do another twelve hours in this cell, but we've decided to let him out early. We've never had anyone take longer than thirty-six hours to turn, so we assume he's okay. It's really important that you don't tell anyone we broke the rules for you, all right?"

Vicky nodded, but she didn't miss that he'd changed the subject.

"It could cause chaos if anyone found out."

Pins and needles ran a debilitating buzz down the back of Vicky's right leg when she got to her feet. She let her left leg hold her weight and watched as Hugh unlock Flynn's cell. It opened with a loud *crack*.

After he'd opened the door, Vicky shoved him aside, rushed in, and hugged the slim Flynn. The journey from their containers to Home had taken it out of both of them, and Flynn's usually robust frame felt lightweight in comparison. The boy also stank. Not even allowed a shower, he'd washed with a bucket and water in his cell but nothing else. Not that Vicky cared; she kept a tight hold on him and inhaled his sweaty funk for a few more seconds before she finally pulled away, a grip on the top of each of his arms. "We made it, Flynn. We made it."

Bags sat beneath the boy's sunken eyes. So deep in their sockets, it gave him a hollow stare. He looked to have aged in the time since Vicky had left him buried alive. The traces of the boy he used to be had all but vanished.

"Did you manage to find out what the alarm was about?" he finally said.

"You know what? I didn't."

When Vicky spun around to ask Hugh, he'd gone. Something about the way he'd acted when she asked about the alarm didn't ring true. But it didn't matter at that moment; Vicky would get to the bottom of it before long.

# Chapter Two

"How odd," Vicky said as she looked one last time for Hugh. "I thought he'd at least stay to show us around."

Flynn returned a vacant expression. On the edge of exhaustion, he looked like he had to be very careful in how he spent his energy.

As she tugged on his arm, Vicky said, "Come on, let's go to my room and see what we can find for you from there."

Vicky led the way down the long corridor and Flynn followed behind. The tired drag of his feet whooshed over the blue linoleum floor as he walked a few steps back from her.

Just before they reached the kitchen area, Flynn said, "What's that smell?"

"Bleach."

Another sniff and Flynn screwed his face up. "I don't like it."

"Strong, isn't it?"

"Why would they use it?"

"To keep the place clean. Bleach kills germs, and you want to do everything you can to keep disease and germs away in somewhere like this. Hospitals used to smell the same way.

Come on," Vicky said and led them into the kitchen area.

As they walked through the vast space, Vicky watched Flynn's reaction. Used to the kitchen shipping container, his jaw fell loose when he looked around. Several chefs prepared food over in one corner, busily chopping and cooking, the smell of boiling vegetables prominent as the pots and pans belched steam into the air.

While Flynn watched the kitchen, the snap of a chef's knife against a chopping board echoed in the large open area. Vicky's gaze wandered to the medic bay. To look at the single bed and small set of drawers on wheels next to it gripped her stomach with nauseating dread. The woeful provisions meant they had no resources to help anyone with anything major. The bed also had the yellow stains of washed-out blood on it. How many people had bled to death because they couldn't perform a simple operation here?

At the other end of the kitchen, they entered the corridor that led to Vicky's room. It might have looked similar to the corridor with Flynn's cell on it, but it felt warmer somehow. Most of the rooms had been made into bedrooms for the residents, which gave it a more homely feel. The same smell of bleach hung in the air, but Vicky had a lot more tolerance for it than Flynn. Maybe she'd been conditioned, but it smelled clean, and clean saved lives—probably many more than the damn medic bay ever could.

After Vicky had entered her room, she had to step back outside to double-check the number on the door. Seventy-two. It was her room, but it looked different from when she'd last been in it. It had two beds shoved into the tight space instead of one. Her bed remained like she'd left it, but the new bed had a pile of clean clothes on it.

After Flynn followed her in, Vicky walked over to the pile of clothes and found a note. Flynn stepped close to her and Vicky caught a whiff of him. She tried not to react to the boy's tang as she read the letter aloud.

*"Welcome to Home, Flynn. You're here as our guest, so please make yourself comfortable and relax. We want to make sure you have every opportunity to get your strength up while you recover from your journey. We have some clean clothes for you and a towel so you can go and take a shower. We normally only let people shower once a week, on Sunday, but sometimes we allow special privileges in cases like yours. Get washed up and we're sure you'll feel a whole lot better. Anyway, please rest and let us know if we can help you at all."*

Once Vicky had finished reading the letter, she lifted the pile of clean clothes. Tracksuit bottoms, a T-shirt, sweatshirt, underwear and socks had been piled up neatly for him. Every item of clothing had the same grey colour. Vicky wore something similar, as did many people in the community. It seemed that those in positions of power dressed slightly smarter with trousers and shirts, but for most people in Home, they wore the grey tracksuit as their uniform.

After she'd passed Flynn the soft pile of clothes, Vicky said, "Want me to show you to the shower block?"

Flynn nodded.

\*\*\*

"Don't worry, they'll get bored soon," Vicky said as she leaned close to Flynn while they walked. About fifty people had gathered in the canteen for lunch, and all of them stared over at Flynn like they had done with Vicky when she'd first arrived.

Vicky watched Flynn's wide eyes dart around the room, clearly self-conscious because of the attention and seemingly afraid to look back at anyone.

On their way to a table, Vicky stopped dead while Flynn continued on. The attention shifted from Flynn to her and her voice echoed in the large canteen. "Come on, guys, give him a break. He's been here two minutes and you're all staring at him. You'll get a chance to meet him, but just let him settle in first, yeah?"

Although a berating, those in the canteen took it well and almost every face turned away from the pair. Vicky walked over to the table in the corner Flynn had chosen to sit down at. "You wait here, and I'll get you some food."

Vicky returned with two steaming bowls of stew. They smelled like overcooked vegetables. For all the chefs there were in Home, none of them seemed able to make anything other than bland sustenance. Although, Vicky would take bland sustenance over no sustenance any day.

The polished tabletop put up little resistance when Vicky slid Flynn's spoon to him, and she flinched in anticipation of the loud noise it would make when it hit the floor. But Flynn caught it before it fell and dipped it into his stew. The boy—obviously still in shock—moved like a machine with a haunted stare in his glazed eyes.

After she'd spooned in a bland mouthful of the watery slop, Vicky said, "We're safe here, you know?"

Flynn stared at her.

"The diseased can't get us."

As Flynn looked at the canteen with a slow turn of his head, he said, "The diseased can't, but *they* can."

And he had a point. At least they could predict what the diseased would do: run and try to kill you. But over a hundred people—all with their own agenda and their own insecurities—could do countless things. To live in such close proximity with strangers required a level of trust that Flynn and Vicky barely had with one another, let alone people they didn't know.

As if stepping forward from the place he'd retreated into within his mind, Flynn stared at Vicky with accusation. "And what about when you get bored?"

"Huh?"

"Like at the containers. You got bored of us and wanted to move on."

"I got bored of the life, Flynn; that's a very different thing."

"Different how?"

"I didn't want to be the spare part anymore. I'd been a clinger on to your family for a decade and I couldn't continue to do it. It got depressing knowing I would never meet anyone new. Besides, I told you when I wanted to move on; I didn't just leave you in the lurch."

A shrug of his shoulders and Flynn spooned another mouthful of stew in. As he looked around the vast canteen—the monitors on the wall showing nothing happening outside—he sighed. "I still think you'll find a reason to move on. I don't think you like responsibility."

The words stung because of the truth within them. Vicky had been distant at the containers. The supply runs were her thing and she could do them easily, but when it came to connecting with other people, she struggled, preferring to retreat to her container rather than open her heart to a fulfilling relationship like a normal human being.

When she looked up at Flynn, she met his dark glare for a second before she looked back down at the white Formica table. "You're right, I did struggle. All I can promise you is that I'll try harder here. Maybe my need to move on from the containers was down to my desire to open up. I finally want to meet new people."

"Or a new person? Is this all because you want to fuck someone?"

Heat flushed Vicky's cheeks. "It's a bit more complex than that, Flynn." It felt strange to talk to him about these things. As hard as she tried not to see him in that way, whenever she looked at the young man, she still saw the little boy sat in the back of the police car as they raced away from his school ten years ago. "Well …" But before she could finish, Vicky caught sight of Hugh, Jessica, and another man. All three of them wore the khaki uniform of those in positions of authority.

With a grin almost as wide as his face and teeth as white as the walls of the canteen, Hugh strode over to them. "So, how are the newest residents settling in?"

In light of her conversation with Flynn, Vicky's face flushed hot again and her heart fluttered. After a dry gulp, she nodded. "Fine."

Both Vicky and Hugh watched Flynn for a response. When he finally looked up, he nodded and spoke a monotone syllable. "Fine."

Vicky looked over at Jessica by the entranceway to one of the corridors. Hugh laughed. "She's not that bad, you know."

"Huh?"

"Your face when you look at Jessica. I know she can be a bit cold—"

Vicky tried to relax her unconscious scowl. "A bit?"

"Okay, so she's our resident ice queen, but she means well. She always wants to do the right thing, even if she doesn't always manage it. Besides, when you get to know her, she really shows you her big heart. Her exterior coldness is a defence mechanism. Trust me, you'll become friends with time."

Her ponytail pulled back so tight it looked like it could scalp her, Jessica kept her eyes fixed on one place as if to look over the heads of everyone in the canteen. Her mouth remained pulled tight in a bitter grimace. A sentry looking for trouble, she'd end it in a heartbeat. Zero tolerance. Zero compassion.

In contrast, the man next to her had dark skin and a warm set to his features. "And who's that?"

"That's Serj," Hugh said. "A lovely guy, he and Jessica have been an item for years now."

Serj stood with his eyes aglow, and although he didn't smile, his face beamed radiance as if he drank in every moment of his life and loved it. Vicky instantly liked him. Although he looked deceptively young, Vicky would have put him at around the same age as Jessica. They both looked to be in their mid-thirties.

When Flynn spoke, his words shot out of him and Vicky jumped. "What was the alarm sound?"

The question caught Hugh off guard and he stepped back a pace. "I told Vicky; it was a test. We need to make sure they work every once in a while. Let's hope we never have to evacuate, but it doesn't do us any harm to prepare, does it?"

Although Hugh had returned Flynn's question with one of his own, Flynn only responded with a cold and narrowed glare.

"Anyway," Hugh said and hooked a thumb over his shoulder, "I need to be off now."

Before either Vicky or Flynn could speak again, Hugh spun around and weaved through the tables in the canteen on his way back to Serj and Jessica.

Once he'd gotten out of earshot, Flynn shook his head. "I don't trust him."

"Why not?"

"He's hiding something."

If Vicky could have argued the point, she would have, but he did seem to be hiding something from them. "Maybe he has a good reason to."

There seemed to be little conviction in Flynn's voice when he said, "Maybe."

# Chapter Three

Having spent several hours in the canteen, many of them in silence as Vicky and Flynn watched the monitors and the other people around them, the pair returned to their sleeping quarters.

The corridor had the usual stink of bleach that caused Vicky to involuntarily ruffle her nose against its probing reach. "I didn't get it at first," Vicky said.

With his feet dragging as he walked, Flynn looked up at Vicky but didn't respond.

"The monitors in the canteen," she continued. "I thought they desensitised the children of the community to the diseased outside."

Although Flynn still said nothing, he watched Vicky.

"But now I get it. I mean, in a world with no windows, those monitors provide some kind of connection with life. The bulbs in this place may be UV, but if nothing else, we need to *see* the outside world, right? We need to at least have an understanding of the sun in the sky, even if we don't feel the warmth of it on our skin. I mean, what do we have without that?"

A few seconds passed as Flynn watched Vicky and he looked like he would respond. Instead, he shrugged and stared ahead again as they drew close to their room.

\*\*\*

Vicky stopped before she opened the door. "Are you sure you're okay sleeping in with me? I can ask them to give you your own room if you like?"

A frown darkened Flynn's face and he spoke in a gruff voice. "Do you want me to sleep on my own?"

Still clearly damaged from everything that had happened over the past week or two, Vicky reached across and touched Flynn's wiry forearm. "I don't mind what you do, honey. I like having you in with me, so stay as long as you like. I just want to make sure you feel comfortable."

With his attention dropped to the floor, Flynn said, "I'll stay for a while. If that's okay?"

"Of course."

When Vicky pushed the door open, it crashed into one of the beds in the room. A small room, it now had two cot beds in it like the ones used by the army or in impromptu hospitals. They had white bedding and silver metal frames. They creaked at any slight movement. Since they'd been out of the room, a clean tracksuit had been left on each bed.

Flynn walked over and lifted his tracksuit up. "I've only just put on fresh clothes. Surely this is a mistake."

A smile lifted Vicky's face as she shook her head. "It's no mistake. Every day you leave your old clothes on the floor and someone comes around and picks them up. At the end of each day, you come back to your room to find a fresh set waiting for you, grundies and all."

A red hue spread across Flynn's face at the mention of underwear, so Vicky spared him the details about the uncomfortable bras. Not that she should complain; she'd often found it difficult to get a well-fitted bra on an entire high street in the past. The fact that Home had something that came close to fitting her had been a miracle.

The space between the beds showed a strip of blue linoleum floor. Too narrow for the pair to pass one another in the tight passage, they'd be lying so close they'd be able to reach across the gap.

White walls and a white ceiling, lit up by the naked bulb, finished off the plain room.

When Vicky sat down on her bed, the springs groaned as they sagged beneath her weight. She rocked from side to side and the entire bed moved with her, the joints creaking with every shift. "Okay, so these aren't the best beds in the world, but they sure beat sleeping on the cold floors of those fucking containers." For some reason, the swear word struck Vicky more than it had done in the past. Her swearing aloud started off as something to get under Larissa's skin, but now they'd joined a community, she had the judgement of close to one hundred other people around her. "I won't miss the airport, will you?"

A shake of his head and Flynn sat down on his creaky bed.

Both beds had a floor space at the foot of them. At about a metre square, they gave some room for Vicky and Flynn to place their personal belongings—if they ever gathered any personal belongings, that was. Maybe when the need for them arose, they could put shelves up.

After Vicky had slipped beneath the covers, she stripped down to her knickers, bra, and vest and tossed the rest of the clothes onto the floor space at the end of the bed.

Once Flynn had settled into bed, Vicky, who had the light switch close to her head, reached up and turned the light out. With the door to the room closed, the place fell into almost complete darkness. Just a sliver of light peeked beneath the door from the hallway.

\*\*\*

As they lay in the dark, Vicky's mind raced, but she kept her thoughts to herself. Flynn would need the rest. From what he'd been through and his time in the cell, he'd ended up looking like the walking dead, and it wouldn't be fair to drag him into a conversation when he should be sleeping.

"Are you asleep?" Flynn said.

Relieved at the break in silence, Vicky said, "No."

"I wonder what the alarm was for?"

"So do I. I really want to trust Hugh and I'm sure we'll find out soon enough what it was about. There's probably nothing to it."

A non-committal grunt and Flynn said, "I hope you're right. I struggle to trust anyone who smiles that much."

"He comes from a different place than us; he's been safe for years. He has more of a reason to be happy than we do."

"I still don't like it."

Neither did Vicky, but Flynn had a lot to deal with already, so she kept it to herself.

The spareness of the room took Flynn's clearing of his throat and amplified it. "I used the spear, you know."

"To get out of the hole?" Vicky asked.

The silence seemed to last an age before Flynn finally said, "Yeah. I had it with me as the tunnel collapsed and I managed to hold onto it with one hand. I couldn't breathe at first and couldn't open my eyes for the damp earth, but I gritted my teeth and wiggled the pole until the smallest amount of daylight came in from above me. I wiggled it some more and it brought in some fresh air with it. I was already knackered by that point."

The guilt of leaving him stabbed pain through Vicky's chest. If Rhys and Larissa could speak to her now, they'd no doubt be furious at how she'd abandoned their son—and rightly so.

"I waited until I got my strength back and I wiggled the pole some more. Slowly but surely, the hole above me grew. I mean, maybe it was a blessing that it took me a while to get out. It gave the diseased enough time to get bored of waiting for me and to fuck off. So when I finally crawled out of the ground, exhausted and covered in dirt, I didn't have to face a whole herd of the bastards."

"I'm so sorry I left you, Flynn."

Another loaded pause seemed to suck all of the air from the room. "It's okay. If you'd have known I was still alive, you would have waited for me. What else could you do but assume I'd died?"

Vicky let him continue.

"I picked up the trail quite easily after that. I mean, the signs are pretty clear, right?"

Vicky laughed. "Right."

"I panicked when I came to the stream."

A sharp gasp and Vicky clapped her hand to her mouth. "Shit, I hadn't even thought about that. How did you cross it?"

"I made a raft. I found a couple of plastic barrels caught in the reeds and fished them out. I used the weeds to bind them to some wood and it took my weight. I managed to push out across the stream just as a herd of the diseased appeared. I got lucky there; if they'd arrived any earlier, I would have either drowned trying to swim across or been bitten."

Despite the fact that Flynn lay next to her now, washed, cleaned, and fed, the pain of the loss of him remained with Vicky and her eyes itched with tears. A sniff did little to clear her running nose.

"Are you okay, Vicky?"

"Yep, I'm fine." A deep breath eased her taut lungs and she added, "I promise, Flynn, I won't give up on you again. I'm so, so sorry."

So dark in the room that Vicky couldn't see his movement, she flinched when Flynn reached over and held her hand. Larger than hers, and always surprisingly strong, Vicky squeezed it back.

The pair remained that way as they drifted off to sleep.

# Chapter Four

The aches of an early morning gripped Vicky's body as she opened her eyes and stared up into the darkness of their room. It would be a while before she felt rested after a night in a nearly comfortable bed. The windowless room made it impossible to tell the time of day, but she had no more sleeping in her. After a deep inhale and a sigh, she heard Flynn shift next to her, the springs groaning their protest at his movement.

"You awake, Vicky?"

Vicky flicked the light switch and watched Flynn recoil as if the glare could cause him harm. After he'd ducked beneath his duvet, he spoke again, his voice muffled by the bedding. "You could have warned me you were going to do that."

It was impossible for her not to smile. Vicky waited for him to reappear and swallowed against the funky taste of morning in her mouth.

When he poked his head out again, Vicky grinned at his dishevelled hair. "Have you been awake long?"

A shake of his head and Flynn stared back at her. "You?"

"No, not long. I'm not sure I can lie in for any longer though."

"Why hasn't anyone asked us to do anything? Surely there's plenty of work that needs to be done in a place like this."

"I think we'll get jobs," Vicky said. "But I get the impression they want to let us get our strength up first. I don't know about you, but too long lounging around without purpose will drive me nuts."

At that moment, Vicky sat up. Although she kept her covers on her, she suddenly felt aware of being dressed in a vest and knickers. They'd spent so much time together it felt like they were related, but they weren't. She should cover up around the young man.

Clearly unable to look over, Flynn blushed, got out of bed, and picked up Vicky's clothes for her. Just before he tossed them onto her bed, Vicky shook her head. "Can you give me yesterday's tracksuit?"

When Flynn turned a puzzled look on her, she shrugged. "I've heard there's a couple of rooms with gym equipment. I've run nearly every day for the past decade, so if nothing else, that's what I need to do now. Wanna come?"

The apathy of a teenager came back at Vicky with Flynn's gentle shrug, and Vicky couldn't help but laugh. She slipped her tracksuit bottoms on beneath the covers and hopped out of bed. "Come on, let's go."

\*\*\*

The reek of bleach accompanied Vicky and Flynn's walk to the gym. They'd passed through the medic bay-slash-kitchen area, and Vicky had watched Flynn's wonder again as he looked around the cavernous space with his jaw hanging loose. The sheer size of Home certainly stood in stark contrast to the understated entranceway, and it had taken Vicky a few trips through the place to get over the vastness of it.

They entered the corridor with the gym room on it and Vicky heard the repetitive *boom, boom, boom, boom* of someone on a treadmill. If there had been any doubt as to where to find the room, the sound had just erased it.

The gym had no door on it, so the second they got level with it, Vicky saw Hugh on the treadmill. Tall and strong, he stared straight ahead, his face glistening with sweat as he pounded away on the machine. A glance at Vicky and he flashed her his brilliant white grin.

When Vicky looked into the next room along, she saw it had free weights in it. One room for cardio, one for muscle building. Not that she'd spend much time muscle building.

Vicky returned to the room with the machines and Flynn followed her in. Although the tang of bleach battled the heady funk of stale sweat, it didn't quite overpower it. The room smelled like an old gym bag.

To be fair to Hugh, he clearly tried to look Vicky in the eye when she removed her sweatshirt, but for the briefest second, his stare ran the length of her body in her tight-fitting vest.

After Vicky had placed her clean clothes on the floor in a pile next to the ones she'd just taken off, she got onto the treadmill next to Hugh and set it at a slow pace to start with. She didn't need to prove anything.

Once she'd settled into a gentle rhythm, she focused on her breath to keep it level and watched Flynn get on the exercise bike in front of the treadmills.

For the first few minutes, none of them spoke. Fixed stares straight ahead accompanied heavy breaths and the whir or thud of the machines. The hard floor and walls amplified every sound in the small space.

Vicky had seen the writing when she'd entered the room. Quotes and mantras written in black on the yellowing walls, Vicky read a few aloud as she ran. "I'm not where I need to be, but thank fuck I'm not where I was."

A wry smile and Hugh forced the words out through his heavy breaths. "I replaced the word 'god' with fuck. I'm not anti-religion or anything, but it's just not my bag, you know?"

Instead of replying, Vicky read the next quote, grinning as she said it, "Fitness: A lifestyle with no finish line."

From the look on Hugh's face, he took the jibes in the good humour Vicky had intended. "They may seem ridiculous to you now, but when you spend ten years here, it's little things like those quotes that make the difference."

A nod at the man and Vicky turned the speed up on her treadmill until the red LCD letters on the screen had turned to seven point zero. When she looked across at Hugh's machine, she saw he had it set to eleven.

About thirty seconds later, Vicky went from seven point one up to eight point five. The click of each increment grabbed Hugh's attention, who looked across at the machine with a raised eyebrow.

As if caught up in the competition, Flynn pedaled faster.

Several more beeps later and Vicky had gone up to level ten. After a few days' rest, her lungs felt tight and her legs ached, but she'd been here many times before, and when she'd had the diseased on her tail, she had to push through it. Once she got past the pain, she could run forever. Although, getting through to the other side seemed harder when she didn't have a pack of rotting diseased behind her.

A few more beeps and Vicky got up to eleven next to Hugh. The pair fell into a natural rhythm, their feet beating against the treadmill in unison, their ragged breaths mirroring one another's. They both stared straight ahead. At that speed, to look down would upset Vicky's balance and she'd be flung into the wall and the stupid quote that read *I think I like who I am becoming*. A collision with that would undermine the statement in an instant.

The vigorous exercise allowed no room for conversation. Still, Flynn said, "When will you tell us about the alarm, Hugh?"

Unflinching as he stared straight ahead, Hugh took a few seconds before he replied. "You're right to be suspicious about the alarm. There is more to it than we've let on. But instead of explaining it—" he fought to get his breath back "—let me show you the next time we need to set it off."

"Do you set it off often?" Flynn asked.

"No. Thankfully."

The reply silenced Flynn, and the tension in the room thickened. What did he mean by that?

It upset Vicky's balance to look across at Flynn, but she did it anyway and met his wide-eyed glare. He clearly wanted some kind of response.

"I trust you, Hugh," she said. Not that she did, but Hugh didn't need to know that. A glance back at Flynn and Vicky saw his eyes had stretched even wider. "Whatever it is, we can wait until you're ready to show it to us."

Flynn stopped cycling, got off the exercise bike, picked up his clean set of clothes, tutted at Vicky, and left the room.

A couple of minutes passed before Hugh said, "What's his problem?"

Hot from the run, Vicky dragged lungfuls of air into her body and ran her arm across her brow to clear the sweat. "He doesn't trust you and he doesn't think that I should either."

Several beeps and Hugh slowed his treadmill down to nine point five. "But you do, right?"

Vicky followed his lead and also slowed down. Pain spread through her chest as she fought to pull in all of the oxygen she needed. "Yeah, I think so."

What else could she say? She would watch him closely. Any sign of wrongdoing and she'd leave Home in a flash, but Hugh didn't need to know that.

After a pause, Hugh said, "So why did you come to the gym today?" The grin on his face looked like he thought Vicky came because of him.

A shake of her head and Vicky laughed; the male ego never ceased to amaze her. "I came because I have nothing to do in my room."

"That's because you need to rest."

"Maybe, but I haven't rested in over a decade, so it's not something that comes easily for me. I haven't been inside for this amount of time in over a decade either. I suppose it's making me antsy. I need to do something."

"If only everyone used that method to deal with their pent-up energy."

"Huh?"

Hugh batted the comment away with his hand. "So how about you join us on the Home guards?"

"No."

"You don't even want to think about it?"

"Sure I do, but I promised Flynn I'd stay by his side. I left him once; I'm not prepared to do it again."

"But he'll be safe in Home. Nothing can break in."

"Even if you're right, I'm not sure I could deal with other people's bullshit. If it was just a case of fighting and working, then I could do it, no problem, but it's dealing with the drama of this place. I'm not sure I could cope with that. And I don't want to work with Jessica."

Now they'd slowed down, Hugh seemed to have more energy. After he'd thrown his head back in a laugh, he said, "That's a fair point about the politics of this place; it does get tiring. Although, Jessica's all right. You just need to give her a chance."

Before Vicky could reply, Hugh cut her off, "And you get one of our sexy uniforms."

Vicky laughed this time. "Well, that's me sold, then! Look, how about I talk to Flynn and we take it from there?" At least if she worked closer to Hugh, she could keep more of an eye on him.

A final beep on Hugh's treadmill and the machine slowed down to a standstill. He then offered his hand for Vicky to shake. "I'll take that deal."

Although sweaty, Vicky took his hand.

# Chapter Five

"So have you thought about what role you might like here?"

Flynn spoke as he scooped up another spoonful of his broth. "Dunno, not really considered it yet."

"Maybe you should."

Flynn didn't respond, a slight wince on his face as he ate.

"I've been having a look at what there is for me to do," Vicky said. "Guard looks like a good option."

Flynn froze, his soup spoon on the way to his mouth again, and he tilted his head to one side. He didn't speak. He didn't need to; his pained accusation said it all.

The stark glare of the boy put Vicky on edge. "I … I, uh, Hugh suggested it and I just thought it might be a good idea, you know. I could do my bit for the community."

To take herself away from his glare, Vicky looked around her. A vast amphitheatre of a room, its floor was littered with tables and chairs. There seemed to be no plan for the layout. And why should there be? Maybe if Home had four times the residents—four or five hundred rather than the one hundred people that lived there—then they'd need to be more organised.

As it stood, the huge place had room to spare. Room for the chaos of disorganisation. Even when everyone in Home gathered in the space, it still looked empty. It painted a sad picture of how ravaged humanity had been by the disease. Ten years and they still barely broke three digits in their number.

When Vicky looked back at Flynn, she found him still staring at her.

"So what else has Hugh asked you to do?"

"What are you suggesting?"

"I've seen the way you look at him."

A few people at a table nearby looked over, and heat flushed Vicky's cheeks. She turned back to Flynn and scowled at the boy. Most of the time she watched Hugh to look for the cracks in his act. If she joined the guards, she could watch him more closely. Not that she could say that in the public space of the canteen. Besides, there seemed no point in making Flynn doubt him too. She didn't have any evidence against his character.

"You said you wouldn't leave me again," Flynn said.

"And I won't. I'll be going out for sure, but I'll be back every day. It'll be just like it was in the containers."

"So I'll sit around doing nothing all day again? Behave like the good little boy I am while you and Hugh run around playing action heroes."

The memories of a decade's worth of encounters with the diseased flashed through Vicky's mind. Sometimes, when she closed her eyes, she saw strobed images as the recollection of the violence blinked through her consciousness. Snapping jaws, bloody mouths, flailing arms … the repeated cracking of skulls as she executed one after another. No matter how she tried, she'd never forget the feeling of their craniums giving way to her blows.

When she spoke to Flynn again, she delivered it with the jab of a pointing finger. "You don't know what I've seen and what I've been through to make sure *you* stayed alive. Do you think it's fun running for your life for the sake of a tin of beans? You think I enjoyed that responsibility? Poor you, having to remain safe for all of those years while everyone else looked after you."

The self-righteous anger that could only come with the inexperience of youth drained from Flynn's tight features and he dropped his gaze to the white table between them.

The brown soup had vegetables in it, and when Vicky took a sip, she tasted rich meat of one sort or another. With no trace of the chewy texture of a dead animal, the stock must have come from a carcass at some point. As she ate, she stared at Flynn, daring him to speak again.

When Flynn drew a breath as if to reply, he opened his mouth and was cut short by the shrill scream of a woman. So high in pitch, it went off like a sonic blast and turned Vicky's spine to ice. Such a violent noise, it sounded all the worse because it didn't belong in the canteen; outside on the battlefield maybe, but not here, not with all the children around. Like a gunshot in a playground, it ran cold dread through Vicky, who spun around to see the woman who'd made the noise.

On her feet, the woman screamed again and slashed at the air between her and a man on the other side of the table from her. "You fucking fuck! What the fuck? You piece of shit."

Wide eyed and red faced, she yelled with such malice spittle shot from her mouth.

"Look, love, I don't know what you're talking about."

The woman stepped up on one of the benches to get to the table and closer to him, a metal butter knife in her hand. "You know everything. You're inside my head, I know it. I hear your voice when I sleep." She knocked against her skull with a clenched fist. "I even hear it during the day. Tormenting me, telling me to do crazy things."

Her voice lifted even higher as she screamed louder than before. "You have no right to be in my head. You need to get the fuck out."

Bowls of soup sat lined up along the table the woman stood on. She kicked each one toward the man as she walked down it.

By that point, Vicky had gotten to her feet. Flynn grabbed her arm as if to stop her, but Vicky shook it off and stepped toward the woman.

A good twenty metres separated Vicky and the crazy woman, so she edged closer as the woman continued. "I've put up with it for too long."

It might only have been a butter knife in her hand, but the woman looked like she could do plenty of damage with it as she waved it in the man's direction. The man had stood up and backed away from her toward one of the corridors that led out of the canteen.

A girl no older than twelve stood between the woman and the retreating man. "Joanne, what are you doing? Harry didn't say anything to you. Why are you having a go at him?"

When Vicky saw the look the woman levelled at the young girl, she took off. She stepped up onto a chair and leaped at one of the several tables between her and the commotion. She sprang from one table and landed on top of another with a loud crash, but even that didn't break the woman's focus on the child.

Vicky jumped down to the floor and swerved around several chairs before she sprang back up onto another table. Just a few metres separated her and the crazy woman, who yelled again and lunged at the young girl, knife first. The girl's scream joined that of the woman's.

Just before the woman made contact, Vicky leaped at her, rugby tackled her around the waist, and knocked the woman from the table down onto the hard floor. Vicky landed on top of her, driving the air from the crazy woman's body with a deep *omph*.

Vicky sat on the woman's chest with her knees on the woman's biceps. The crazed eyes of the lunatic showed a lack of humanity Vicky had only previously associated with the diseased. Lost in the confusion of her own mind, this woman clearly didn't register any human rationality. Something had broken inside of her.

The woman twisted and writhed beneath Vicky's weight, but no matter how she tried, she couldn't throw Vicky from her. After a short while, exhaustion took over and the woman lost some of her fight.

Vicky then felt a hand squeeze her shoulder. When she looked behind her, she saw Jessica flanked by Hugh and Serj. "You can leave her to us now, Vicky. Thank you."

Hugh and Serj moved to either side of the woman and grabbed an arm each. Vicky climbed off her and stared at the dishevelled mess as they dragged her to her feet. Something had permanently switched off inside of the woman, and it didn't look like it would come back any time soon.

The people in the canteen gathered around. All of them stared at the guards as if waiting for them to act. The tension in the air seemed to turn into something else, closer to anticipation than fear. Before Vicky could think on it any further, Hugh leaned close to her and said, "I promised you I'd show you what the alarm was for. Now's the time to find out."

A twinge twisted Vicky's heart as she watched the three guards lead the woman away. She nearly didn't follow the crowd out of the canteen, but she had to know what the alarm meant. As she took up the tail of the pack, she went by Flynn to bring him with her. Nausea churned through her stomach when she said to him, "We're about to find out what the alarm was for."

Flynn's eyes shifted from side to side as they studied Vicky's, but he didn't respond. Instead, he followed her and the rest of the pack from the canteen. They headed for the corridors that led to the front door of Home.

# Chapter Six

Vicky and Flynn followed the rush of people toward the small foyer at the front of Home. Many—if not all—of Home's residents made the hasty pilgrimage, forcing Vicky and Flynn to the back of the crowd.

When they got to one of the sets of stairs that led from the canteen up into the foyer, the crowd bottlenecked and they couldn't get through. Instead, Vicky turned to look at Flynn.

A deep frown stared back at her. "Seems like a lot of fuss for a batty old woman."

Even this far back, the crush of bodies pushed against Vicky. Claustrophobia pulled her chest tight. Whenever she moved, she touched another person, and the collective funk of bodies that only washed once a week turned the air thick with the muddy reek of dirt. "It sure does," she said in response to Flynn. "But you want to know what's going on as much as I do, right?"

Despite their distance from the foyer, the people around Vicky and Flynn craned their necks and pushed and shoved to get an inch or two farther up the stairs. Whatever they were looking for, it seemed impossible to see it from where they stood.

When Vicky heard her name, she froze. It ran down the crowd, passed like a baton from one pair of lips to another.

"Vicky."

"Vicky."

"Vicky."

As it journeyed through different voices and accents, it caught up with Vicky and shot straight past her. She'd not met many people yet, so they wouldn't know her. Vicky called after the name as it ran down the crowd and into the canteen. "I'm here."

As one, the crowd of people stopped and silence descended. For a second, everyone waited. A call then came out from those up in the foyer. "Bring her up."

Although she received many resentful looks, the crowd parted for Vicky, who reached out and grabbed Flynn's hand before she shoved her way up the stairs.

With the bodies packed as tightly as they were, she had to squeeze through the crush. She gripped Flynn's hand hard to make sure they didn't get separated.

At the top of the stairs, the crowd parted more willingly, and Vicky saw Hugh for the first time since he'd dragged the woman away. He still had a hold of the woman, but seemed to be waiting for Vicky before he made his next move.

Another couple of paces and Vicky found herself at the front of the crowd with Flynn. They stood next to Hugh and had a great view out of one of the large windows next to the door.

With a grim frown, Hugh dipped a gentle nod at Vicky that gripped her bowels in an anxious pinch. With so many onlookers, Vicky didn't speak. Instead, she watched Jessica walk up to the large steel door and grab the bolt at the top. She turned to Hugh and Serj, her brows raised questioningly as if double-checking what they wanted her to do. Both Hugh and Serj encouraged her with a stoic nod, and Jessica closed her eyes as if in prayer.

The anticipation in the small room hung so thick Vicky's stomach turned backflips and her heart crashed against her ribcage.

When Jessica opened her eyes, they'd glazed with tears, but she accepted her role in it all by returning a nod to Hugh and Serj. A deep breath and she pulled the top bolt free with a loud *crack*!

The sound of the lock took off over the heads of the dead-silent people in the entranceway, raced down the stairs, and got swallowed by the vast amphitheatre of the canteen below.

When Jessica leaned down for the second bolt at the bottom of the door, a few people in the audience gasped. The sharp hiss of it hit Vicky at the base of her neck and she flinched. Before she could look around to find the source of the sound, the large hinges on the huge steel door creaked as Jessica pulled it open.

The woman who'd lost the plot had been silent, almost sedate in comparison to her anxious state of only minutes earlier. It seemed like Hugh holding her tightly filled her with some kind of calm. But as she watched the large steel door open in front of her, her insanity returned. At first, she shook her head. A few seconds later, her entire body. A few more seconds, and she thrashed and writhed as if she could get free from the men's strong grip.

As she twisted and squirmed, she screamed, "Please don't. *Please*, let me be."

Although Vicky watched the woman, she found herself looking more at Hugh for his reaction. A look passed between him and Serj; then, as one, they stepped forward with the loud woman so they stood just outside of the open doorway.

It almost needed a countdown before they shoved her out, but the men saved the woman that indignity. Instead, they continued to look at one another before Hugh nodded again.

They forced the woman forward with a hard shove and she stumbled out of Home. After a few wobbly steps, she tripped and landed flat on her face.

Both Hugh and Serj withdrew back into the foyer.

Vicky watched on, her throat dry as the door to the complex remained open.

It seemed that Jessica had frozen in place while she watched the woman splayed out on the ground. The woman made no effort to get back in. Instead, she got to her knees, remained hunched over, and sobbed.

When Jessica still didn't move, Hugh shoved her aside and slammed the door shut. Two loud *cracks* echoed as he slid the bolts back into place.

Despite the press of bodies, silence consumed the entranceway. A few people shifted to peer out the windows at the woman.

Hugh, Jessica, and Serj all moved over to a window. Hugh moved to the one next to Flynn and Vicky; Jessica and Serj moved over to the other side. Everyone who had a view of her watched the woman outside.

After what seemed to be about a minute or two of sobbing, the broken woman shakily got to her feet. With her hair sticking out at all different angles, she walked through the long grass away from Home. She moved as a drunkard would after leaving the pub, so intoxicated she didn't know which direction to walk in.

She walked with an awkward gait as she looked from left to right, clearly in search of the diseased.

When Vicky felt Flynn press into her side, she put her arm around him.

"What's going to happen to her?" Flynn said.

"Maybe she'll get away."

When Hugh looked down at the pair, a sad regret twisted his features, and fear gripped Vicky's heart.

A huge red button sat above the door. Vicky hadn't noticed it before, but it seemed so obvious now as Hugh reached up to it. Before he hit it, he spoke loud enough for everyone to hear. "May your journey be as painless as possible."

A murmur of "Amen" came from the crowd surrounding them.

When Hugh hit the large button, the wet throb of the alarm called out. The same sound they'd heard before, it rang loud in the foyer, but it seemed louder outside.

At the noise, the woman stopped, almost like she'd given up at that point.

Before Vicky could say anything to Hugh, Flynn gasped next to her. Five diseased—all moving with their clumsy sprint— rounded the corner and came straight for the woman.

Before Vicky had time to even catch her breath, they'd crashed into the woman and knocked her to the ground.

For a moment, Vicky couldn't see the woman for the bodies

that dived on top of her, their faces leaning down and coming back up a second later covered in blood.

Then, as quickly as it had started, the diseased pulled back from the woman and left her twitching and bloody form lying on the ground.

Vicky looked from the fallen woman to Hugh and saw the grim set of his face. Horror had turned Vicky's entire being slack at what she'd witnessed. Not so with Hugh. He didn't seem to derive any pleasure from it, but he did condone what had just happened. Hell, he'd instigated it.

Before Vicky could say anything, a young boy in the gathered crowd said, "Oh no."

It started as the woman's arm snapping away from her fallen form. It kicked away from her body as if a jolt of electricity snapped through her. Then the other arm twitched. Seconds later the woman's legs shook, spasming and twisting as she went through the bizarre animation process that turned a normal human into a diseased.

The woman then jumped to her feet. As if driven by the memory of what had happened to her, she sprinted back toward Home. In spite of the thick glass and steel door, Vicky heard her harpy scream. With her mouth stretched wide, her eyes bleeding, and fury driving her on, she ran straight for the window in front of Vicky.

The woman collided with the transparent barrier with a huge *boom* that drove Vicky—and several of the crowd around her—back. Vicky then watched as the woman pressed her face into the glass. The woman's bloody lips pulled as she dragged a red line down the other side of the clear pane. The chink of her teeth tapped against the transparent barrier, almost as if she thought she could bite through to them.

After a few minutes of watching the woman, Vicky turned around to see most of the people that had gathered around her had gone. They'd seen the woman's death; they seemed satisfied in some bizarre way. Maybe they'd seen the horror show so frequently, they didn't need to watch any more.

When she shared another look with Hugh, Vicky shook her head at him, genuinely at a loss for words.

Hugh then left and followed the rest of the people, leaving just Flynn and Vicky remaining in the entranceway.

In the near silence, punctuated only by the woman's growls and hisses on the other side of the glass, Flynn said, "What kind of place is this?"

Strung out with anxiety, Vicky shook her head. "I'm not sure, mate. But I don't fucking like it."

# Chapter Seven

The next morning, Vicky walked down the bleach-infused corridor toward the gym. She carried her clean clothes under her arm to change into after she'd worked out.

The boom of someone's feet accompanied the whine of a treadmill spinning close to maximum speed. It could have been anyone in there, but more than likely it would be Hugh. He seemed more obsessed than most with working out.

A stale funk of sweat hung in the air of the gym like it always did, and whether it came directly from Hugh or not, Vicky couldn't help but attribute it to him.

After Vicky had stepped onto the spare treadmill, she dropped her clean clothes on the floor and set the machine to a fast walk at number seven.

Before long, she'd picked up to eleven, like Hugh next to her. The pair hadn't yet said a word to one another, and although Vicky felt Hugh look across at her from time to time, she continued to stare straight ahead.

The quote—one that she'd read the last time she'd visited the gym—stared back at her. Black on the yellowing walls, she finally spoke as she read it aloud, "I think I like what I am becoming."

The thud of her feet played in time with Hugh's, and he didn't reply.

Vicky slowed back down to seven and looked across at the man, red-faced and covered in sweat. "Do you? A murderer. A savage!"

A large red button sat in the centre of the running machine's console as an emergency stop. Hugh slapped his palm against it with a loud *thwack*. The machine slowed to a halt and he turned to face Vicky, panting as he looked across at her. "What's that supposed to mean?"

"Flynn and I spoke last night. Now we've seen what you do to people here, we're thinking of leaving. I said to Flynn I'd come and talk to you, just to give you a chance to explain your murdering ways before we make our final decision."

As Hugh fought for breath, he shook his head at Vicky. "You've got it all sussed out, eh? What would you do with someone in that state?"

"I'd lock them up until they got better."

"And what if they didn't get better? Or worse, what if we thought they'd gotten better and we let them back into the community, only to find they hadn't improved?"

A glaze covered Hugh's eyes as if he'd retreated into his memories. "Ten years, Vicky," he said. "We've been here for ten years. We've had people lose the plot in that time and we've tried different ways of doing things. But you know what? None of the other ways have worked. And you know what else? People die when we try to look after someone who's lost it. The thing that sends them insane is being in here. Locking them up in a cell isn't going to make them feel any better. I'd rather be"—he used air quotes—"a 'murderer' than put the lives of innocent people at risk. We have children in this place."

Vicky opened her mouth to speak, and Hugh cut her off. "It's sad, don't get me wrong, and Joanne didn't choose to lose her mind, but we're a community, and we have to do what's best for the community. As the leader, I have to make the tough decisions."

"But is the alarm necessary? It seems like a frivolity designed to make a sport of murder."

"Do you know what happens to people when you kick them out of a community?"

A slap against the red button on her treadmill and Vicky walked to a stop. "They get infected by the diseased?" she offered.

"Not always."

"Then what?"

"They get resentful," Hugh said.

"And rightly so. You've kicked them out when they needed help."

"Help that we can't give them. And when someone's resentful, they seek retribution. Several years ago, a man we kicked out hid until we came out of the complex. He took out three of us before we could get him. The alarm makes sure that doesn't happen again."

Hugh picked up a white towel and dabbed at his face and neck with it. "What you saw yesterday is a part of who we are. Sure, it's an ugly part, but it's still who we are. We will never risk the community for the sake of one person."

"So if I lost it, or if Flynn lost it, or Jessica or Serj …"

"We'd kick you out in a heartbeat," Hugh said. "It would be with a heavy heart, but nobody—not even me—is bigger than this community. If you can't accept that, then maybe you should leave."

Before Vicky could reply, Hugh stepped off his treadmill and left the room.

# Chapter Eight

Dressed in a fresh tracksuit, Vicky sat down opposite Flynn in the canteen. The vast space did little for communal spirit. With room to spare, everyone clustered in their own little huddles. Flynn had followed suit by choosing a table in one corner away from everyone else.

The broths they ate most days made the room smell of steamed cabbage. It took Vicky back to her school days of carrots and peas overcooked to the point where they'd had all the colour boiled out of them. But the broths prepared in the kitchen always filled a hole and at least had some flavour.

With a steaming spoon raised to her lips and the meaty smell of the soup lifting into her nostrils, Vicky blew on it. She looked up to find Flynn's eyes on her.

Before she had a chance to take a mouthful, he said, "Well? What happened when you went to see Hugh?"

A sip of the rich broth and Vicky shrugged. "I expected him to be more defensive and ashamed of his actions."

"He wasn't?"

"Not really, no. He said that after running this place for a decade, when someone got to the state of that woman yesterday, the only option they had was to throw them out." Vicky relayed the rest of the conversation to Flynn, especially the part about why they used the alarm.

The twist of youthful indignation slowly melted from Flynn's face as he seemed to see some logic in Hugh's defence of their actions. The certainty left his voice. "It all seems a bit messed up to me."

Another sip of her broth and Vicky nodded. "Of course, but what part of our world isn't?"

As Flynn pushed his empty bowl away from him, he looked at all of the people in the canteen. Maybe fifty people there, at least half were children. "So if it was one of these kids, the same would happen to them?"

"From the way Hugh spoke, he'd want the same to happen to *him* if he lost it. He said it needs to happen for the good of the community. Nothing can jeopardise that. So if we want to stay here, we have to live by those rules. What do you th—"

Before Vicky could finish her question to Flynn, the stamp of boots entered the canteen. Led by Hugh, several guards came into the room. Serj and Jessica stood by either side of him, and another larger man stood behind. Although Vicky had seen the larger man around, she didn't know who he was. He had a deep tan and looked like he could wrestle a bear. She'd heard him speak once or twice. He'd sounded Russian, and Vicky had heard his name was Piotr.

Slightly out of breath from what seemed to be panic rather than exertion, Hugh addressed the room. "We're under attack …"

Although Hugh continued to speak, Vicky lost the rest of his words and her head spun. Since she'd been at Home, she'd lowered her guard from the constant state of high alert she'd lived with over the past decade. She couldn't afford to get complacent.

Vicky's awareness of the room returned in time to see Hugh change channel on the monitors in the canteen. It showed what looked to be the back of the complex. A field with long grass, although not as long as everywhere else, had lines and lines of solar panels. A horde of diseased, larger than she'd seen anywhere outside of the airport, meandered through the space.

"They may not realise they're attacking our energy source," Hugh said, "but they're doing damage. Without power, we won't be able to live down here. We need electricity to circulate the air so we can breathe."

When Vicky looked at Flynn and the strong set of his jaw, she saw it a second before it happened. Flynn stood up and his chair screeched out behind him. It cut through the relative silence of the canteen and most people turned his way. As the only person to stand up, Flynn said, "I'll join you."

As much as Vicky wanted to tell Flynn no, she had to let him make his own decisions. He'd survived through a lot more than most of the people in the community, and she couldn't deprive them of his talents.

Although less enthusiastic, Vicky got to her feet too and locked stares with Hugh.

Silence hung in the canteen for the next few seconds and Hugh looked over the place. Most people averted their gaze by either looking down at their tables or watching the monitors with the pack of diseased on them.

After a shake of his head and a heavy sigh, Hugh nodded at Flynn and Vicky. "Come on, let's go."

As Vicky walked toward Hugh, she watched his sneer of disgust at the rest of the canteen. As clear as his thoughts were about their cowardice, he said nothing to the room.

# Chapter Nine

Hugh stopped at the front door to Home and handed baseball bats to Vicky and Flynn. "I'm afraid it's all we have."

With the bat in her hands, Vicky wrung the grip and shrugged. "Good enough for me." A glance at Flynn and she saw the colour had drained from his angular face. Although he'd filled out a bit since he'd arrived at Home, he currently looked paler and more withdrawn than ever. "You okay?"

When Flynn flashed her the kind of look a child would flash an embarrassing parent, Vicky didn't ask again. He needed to do this without her undermining him.

On their way out of the canteen, Hugh had grabbed a skinny boy of no more than about twelve years old. Although slight, he stood tall for his age. When Hugh nodded at him, the boy snapped the top lock of the door free with a *crack*. A shake took a hold of him as he leaned down to the second one at the bottom. So much for the monitors desensitising them to the threat of the diseased; the boy looked ready to throw up. When the loud *crack* of the second lock snapped through the small entranceway, Vicky's stomach tensed. A deep breath did nothing to ease the grip fear had on her guts. Before she could think on it any further, Hugh led the way and they all stepped outside.

The first time she'd left Home since she'd arrived there, Vicky stood in the open space as the wind crashed into her. The strong breeze buffeted her ears and blew her hair back from her face. The air might have been fresh, but it also had a tinge of rot that lifted the hairs on the back of her neck and set her senses on edge. She'd been here before and she knew just what to do. Regardless of the rest she'd had in Home, a decade of fighting the horrible fuckers had ingrained the warrior spirit in Vicky's psyche.

Hugh led the way around the back of Home and they all followed. The entrance sat embedded in the side of a small hill. A couple of metres' climb and Vicky saw the sea of black that spread away from them. "Wow," she said. "How many solar panels do you have out here?"

"Three hundred and twenty-seven," Hugh replied. "Every one of them still works. It's how we run Home and, second to water and food, it's our most precious resource. I come out here at least once a week to trample the grass so they can get as much sun as possible."

Despite her fascination with the solar panels, Vicky could only look at them for a brief spell. Weaving through the field of black, she saw close to thirty diseased. As she watched the creatures, the wind hit Vicky so hard she had to widen her stance to avoid getting knocked over.

At present, the diseased meandered without focus because they clearly hadn't seen Vicky and her gang. That couldn't last forever.

When Hugh pointed to a grassy mound on their left, Vicky looked at the large elevated patch of grass. A perfect lump, it stood a few more metres taller than its surroundings and it seemed like it had been put there on purpose; like some kind of burial mound. Although, in all probability, it had been a pile of dirt dug from the ground when they built Home. It had now become a prominent pimple on the landscape, as covered in long grass as its surroundings.

"We should get on top of that and defend ourselves," Hugh said. "It's our best chance."

Without another word, Hugh took off and the gang followed.

Vicky ran next to Flynn and checked across once or twice to be sure he seemed okay. Although pale, Flynn had a stubborn set of determination on his boyish features. He'd be all right.

With Jessica, Serj, and the large man on her other side, Vicky focused on the grass mound. A defendable position, they could get to that and have a good chance at taking the fuckers down.

In the blink of an eye, Serj tripped and hit the ground next to Vicky. He yelled out as he fell. When Vicky looked at the diseased, her stomach sank. Where every one of them had stared at their feet as they shuffled through the long grass, they now all looked up at the pack. Dried blood in their eye sockets, dark mouths hanging loose, the horde screamed as one.

Although Serj had fallen, Hugh picked up his pace and yelled at them, "Come *on*, we need to get to the top of that mound to stand a chance."

Jessica stopped to help Serj, but the rest of them carried on.

Vicky looked from the horde to the downed Serj and back to the mound and said, "Fuck it. You go with them, Flynn." She then turned back to help Jessica and Serj.

Jessica had gotten Serj to his feet and the man had his arm around her. He didn't look like he could hold his own weight, and Jessica couldn't fight while she carried him.

"Get Serj to the mound now," Vicky shouted at Jessica. "We can defend him from there."

Fear had left a glaze on Jessica's eyes as she stared at Vicky, but she didn't speak. Instead, she stood frozen for a second.

A glance at the approaching pack and Vicky saw they all headed her way. She turned back to Jessica and shouted, "Get the fuck to that mound. *Now!*"

Jessica set off slowly with Serj toward the others. Vicky rolled her shoulders, raised her baseball bat, swallowed against the dryness in her throat, and drew a deep breath to still her hammering heart. Now the closest to the pack, Vicky found herself to be the focus of the chaotic hive mind heading their way.

## Chapter Ten

Each solar panel had been elevated on short stilts that lifted them to about waist height. The diseased moved as an enraged pack through them. They might have all taken a different route through the gridded maze in a strange, hip-snaking dance, but they all shared one goal: get to Vicky.

With her bat still raised, Vicky stepped back several paces so she stood with the drop of the hill that led down to the front of Home directly behind her.

Just a few metres until the first diseased got to her and Vicky checked to see Jessica drag Serj closer to the group on the mound. They were about halfway between Vicky and the others and needed more time.

The first diseased screamed as it came at Vicky, its mouth spread wide as it issued a long and drawn-out hiss. At the last moment, Vicky darted to the side like a matador avoiding a bull. The diseased steamed past her and fell down the hill on the other side.

Two more came at Vicky. She avoided the first and drove the fat end of her bat into the centre of the face of the second one. It sank into its nose with a wet crack and knocked the creature backwards.

When Vicky looked at the mound again, she saw Jessica help Serj to the top.

Surrounded by the smell of rot and excrement, Vicky hit the next diseased with her bat just as the one she'd already knocked down got to its feet.

Vicky spun sideways to avoid another diseased and spun back the other way to avoid the next one. Both of them stumbled over the top of the hill and fell down the other side.

With the main bulk of the group nearly upon her, Vicky took off toward the mound with the others on it at a flat out sprint.

The group, including Serj, had formed a ring on the mound with their backs to one another. It seemed like a solid plan.

The slathering and out-of-breath pants of the diseased chased on Vicky's heels. She felt the vibration of their footfalls more heavily through the ground with every step. The long grass dragged on Vicky's momentum as she ran, but she gritted her teeth and pushed on with all she had.

The group behind Vicky got so close that the hot reek of rot and shit partially choked her, restricting her breaths into her already tight lungs.

As she got to the bottom of the mound, Flynn jumped from the top, ran past her, and she heard the *tonk* of his baseball bat connecting with a skull.

At the top, Vicky fell into the circle, turned her back to the others as Flynn rejoined them, and wrung the baseball bat in her sweaty grip as she waited for the rest of the pack to catch up.

Vicky didn't know these people like she knew Flynn, but she had to trust them, or at least try to. If anyone got it wrong, they'd be overwhelmed in a heartbeat. Shaking the thought from her mind, Vicky yelled out as she brought her bat down on the crown of the first diseased to come up the small hill at her.

The creature fell. Its legs buckled beneath it and it rolled backwards down the small mound, knocking another diseased over on its way to the bottom.

Cries, screams, and heavy blows lit the air up around Vicky, and as much as she wanted to spin around every time she heard a diseased yell out behind her, she focused on the next one in front and trusted the others. Five to six diseased each; if they killed that many without getting bitten, they'd get out of this mess.

The group stood separately enough from one another that Vicky didn't feel restricted while fighting. But they didn't stand so far apart for the diseased to find holes in their defence. The size of the mound worked out perfectly for them.

The second diseased to come at Vicky received a heavy blow to the bottom of its chin as she drove the bat in an uppercut at it. It had the desired effect and nearly lifted the creature clean off the ground on its way back down the small hill.

A slight lull and Vicky glanced next to her. She froze for the briefest moment when she saw Flynn; he looked more like Rhys than he ever had before. The whites of his eyes glowed in his red and sweating face as he slammed diseased after diseased with his bat. It seemed that half the pack came at him and he drove every one of them back with ease. The little boy she'd known at the containers had well and truly left him.

A scream, no more than a metre away, snapped Vicky's attention back to the diseased running at her. A skinny woman, who would probably have been in her early twenties before she'd turned, sprinted up the hill. With time to jab her bat and nothing else, Vicky drove the diseased woman back with a stab to the face. The woman hit the ground and jumped straight back to her feet.

The second time she came at her, Vicky set herself better, widened her stance, and caught the woman in the temple with a full-bodied swing. A vibration ran up the bat, and in the briefest moment before the monster fell away, Vicky saw her left eye burst from the blow.

After the woman had fallen to the ground, Vicky panted where she stood and looked around. She couldn't see any more diseased, and other than the heavy gasps from their group, she heard nothing.

When Vicky looked at the rest of her party, they all looked back at her and at one another. Had anyone been infected? Did they need to deliver another fatal blow? But no one wore the anxiety of someone hiding a wound. Instead, they returned relieved expressions and even a half smile from Hugh.

Before anyone could speak, Vicky looked at Flynn. The pair shared a nod and both ran down the mound. Hard to tell if any would get back up or not; Vicky and Flynn knew they shouldn't risk it. When she found a diseased that looked unconscious rather than dead, she gripped her bat in both hands and held it so the fat end pointed down. She then released a yell as she drove the bat into the centre of the monster's face. It sank through its skull with a wet squelch and hit the ground beneath it with a thud that ran all the way up into Vicky's tired shoulders.

After she'd wiped some of the sweat from her brow, she looked up to see Flynn do the same to one of the downed monsters next to him.

\*\*\*

It took a little longer for Hugh and Piotr to join Vicky and Flynn down at the bottom of the mound. They too set about attacking the fallen diseased. In a world where mistakes could be fatal, it was always better to be safe. A symphony of squelches from skull after skull being crushed surrounded Vicky as she looked back up the mound at Jessica and Serj. Jessica had returned to holding Serj up. The man sweated more than anyone and looked to be in a lot of pain still.

Once they'd worked through every possible reanimator, Vicky went to Jessica and Serj and let Serj put his other arm around her.

At first, Serj seemed reluctant, but Vicky laughed at him. "There ain't no room for pride in this world anymore. If you're alive, you're winning."

Although he initially frowned at her, Serj nodded and let Vicky help bear his weight as they shifted down the hill.

"I'm sorry," he said as they walked. "When I fell, I twisted my ankle badly and I couldn't do anything. I'm so sorry."

"Do you think it's broken?" Vicky said.

A shake of his head and Serj winced, clearly from his pain. "No." He made Jessica and Vicky stop when he turned to Vicky and hugged her. "Thank you. Thank you so much."

Jessica didn't speak. Instead, she walked over to Vicky and also gripped her in a tight embrace. When she pulled back, Vicky looked into her blue eyes at the stark gratitude of someone still in shock over their near loss. Vicky leaned her head forward and Jessica mimicked her until the two women touched foreheads. In that moment their relationship changed. They then pulled away from one another and bore Serj's weight again as they led him back toward Home.

## Chapter Eleven

Hugh and Piotr strode ahead of Vicky, Flynn, Jessica, and the injured Serj. They did it under the guise of making sure the way was clear, but it conveniently took them closer to the safety of Home too. For all of Hugh's bravado, he could get infected as easily as anyone could, and he'd already proven he would leave people behind to save himself.

As Vicky and Jessica helped Serj down the small but steep hill, the strong wind battered them and made walking unstable. Despite squinting, the fierce gales still made Vicky's eyes water. With a grip around Serj's waist, she used her other hand to keep his arm in place around her neck. They had to get him back inside as quickly as they could.

Although Jessica fought for breath once they'd reached the bottom of the hill, she still managed to force her words out. "I know I've already said it, but thank you for helping me save Serj. We'd both be dead were it not for you."

The humbling experience seemed to have banished Jessica's ice queen persona.

Before Vicky could respond, a scream ran across the open

space and she snapped alert. The sound came from in front of Piotr and Hugh and it bore down on them like an owl on a mouse.

Anxiety flipped Vicky's stomach and turned her mouth arid as she watched both Hugh and Piotr freeze in the face of the diseased's onslaught.

Just before Vicky let go of Serj, Hugh sprang to life, screamed back, and ran straight at the lone diseased figure to meet it head-on. He hit the large man with a heavy whack of his bat, swinging so hard it spun Hugh around after he'd connected, and he stumbled to the point of nearly falling. It knocked the monster down, but the diseased remained active as it writhed on the ground. Hugh stood over it with his bat raised again and used both hands to bring it down on the diseased's head. The creature screamed in reaction to the attack. A wet squelch cut it dead and silence followed, a silence so complete, even the wind seemed to hold its breath.

Hugh panted for a few seconds before he looked in Vicky's direction and raised a thumb at them. He could have simply looked in Vicky's direction and nothing more than that, but in that moment, it seemed that he looked straight at her. Almost as if to prove he could do the right thing.

\*\*\*

The same skinny twelve-year-old boy Hugh had put on the door to Home opened it for the gang when they returned. Vicky, Jessica, and the wounded Serj took up the rear, and once they'd entered, the boy slammed the door behind them and cracked both locks into place.

In the heat of the moment, Vicky hadn't noticed it. And maybe it would have taken longer had the boy not stared at her, clearly horrified, his features hanging slack. But now that she stood in the safety of Home, Vicky felt the weight of her clothes. Soaked in the fetid blood of the diseased, she felt like a walking biohazard.

Were the canteen not the first place she had to enter to get to her room, then Vicky would have taken another way round and avoided the crowd completely. If the place didn't have so many people in it, then maybe she would have walked through there in just her underwear. Currently, she could do neither, so she kept her bloody clothes on and she continued to help Jessica lead Serj down the stairs.

Although Hugh, Piotr, and Flynn slowed down for the wounded member of their party, they still entered the canteen moments before Vicky, Jessica, and Serj. The roar of what sounded like the entire community nearly knocked Vicky backwards when she followed them in a second later, and she looked at the open joy focused on her.

A couple of young teenagers rushed over with a chair and gave it to Serj, who nodded his thanks and winced as he sat down on it.

Unable to hear much over the celebration, Vicky accepted a hand wash from two older women. The women said nothing as they cleaned her, and once they'd finished, they passed her two biscuits and a bottle of water, dipped nods at her, and backed away.

The wash of noise in the high-ceilinged canteen spun Vicky out and made her dizzy. It took for Hugh, who chewed on one of the biscuits given to him by the community, to stand on his chair and cut the air with a chop of his hand. The crowd responded and the sound died down.

As Vicky watched the leader of the community stand tall and strong on the chair—his thick arms folded across his chest, enhancing his already large upper body—she bit into one of the biscuits given to her. The sweet and crumbly texture made her salivate, and, unable to control her impulse, she put the entire thing in her mouth.

Once the crowd's chatter had completely died down, Hugh let the silence hang for a few seconds, a half smile raising one side of his mouth before he finally shouted, "We did it!"

As he thrust his arms in the air—a grin as wide as his handsome face beaming—the crowd went crazy again.

What felt like a minute or two later, the noise died down in anticipation of Hugh's speech.

"So, in case anyone hasn't met them yet, I'd like to introduce you all to Home's newest residents."

Vicky's stomach did a backflip when Hugh turned to her and Flynn, and Piotr's gentle hand urged her forward. Although reluctant, Vicky stepped toward their leader on his chair, Flynn by her side.

Before she got to the man, she chewed on her second biscuit, and it turned into a paste in her dry mouth. A couple of panicked gulps and it felt like the food could stick in her throat. She didn't need to be choking in front of the entire place. A sip of water helped, but it still hurt to swallow the lump. Another sip and Vicky cleared her throat of the bulk of it before she arrived next to Hugh, sweat raised beneath her collar from the panic. A chair appeared on either side of Hugh from some of the children in Home, and Vicky and Flynn stepped up onto them next to their leader.

Despite her urge to punch him for dragging her up there, Vicky smiled at Hugh and then checked Flynn. The boy seemed to be loving the attention, a chance to be a hero in a world where he'd been constantly disempowered. To see his joy made it slightly easier for Vicky to stand up next to him.

"Ladies and gentlemen, boys and girls, I'd like to introduce Flynn and Vicky to you."

The crowd erupted once more and the high ceiling filled with the collective swirl of celebration.

Hugh cut them off with another chop of his hand, and a slight sneer lifted his lip. Accusation rode his words. "These are people we need to keep in Home. They're prepared to fight for us. There will be times when we need it again. Please consider it next time because we may not be so lucky to return if so few of us are prepared to go out."

Silence fell on the place and tension gripped Hugh's frame. He looked ready to say more, so Vicky reached across and squeezed his thick arm. A heavy sigh and he dipped his head as if to reset his thoughts before he looked back up again. "But let's not dwell on that. I think you'll all agree that Vicky and Flynn are amazing."

The crowd—less enthusiastic for being reprimanded—still made encouraging noises.

"And why wouldn't you? You saw everything on the monitors, right? You saw the hero that this woman is when she put her own life on the line to make sure Jessica could get Serj to safety."

The crowd stirred more than before.

"Well, I saw this in Vicky before we went out, and I've already asked her to be my deputy. Jessica has expressed an interest to work more closely with Serj, so I need someone to help me with the day-to-day running of this place. I need a woman like Vicky by my side."

Although Vicky felt Hugh look at her, she kept her attention on the floor and waited for more.

"So I'm going to ask her again."

Vicky looked up at the excited Hugh.

"Vicky," he said, "will you be my deputy and help me run Home?"

How could she trust Hugh after he'd left Serj behind? But then she looked up, and not only did she see hope on the faces of the citizens of Home—from the small children to the adults older than her—but she also saw respect. Besides, she'd been pretty certain she'd do it before she'd gone out to fight with Hugh and the others. A glance at Flynn, and the boy smiled and nodded at her. They'd found a place they could settle down in, even if Hugh did need a few lessons in courage.

A heavy sigh and Vicky looked up at the crowd again before she finally said, "Yeah, okay."

The sound damn near knocked Vicky off the seat she stood on. After she'd raised an appreciative wave at the residents of Home, she stepped down as they continued to cheer.

Before Vicky could catch her breath, Jessica came over, wrapped her in a tight hug and whispered in her ear, "I'm so pleased you said that. Welcome to Home. You're a hero."

# Chapter Twelve

Dressed in the khaki shirt and trousers of a guard, Vicky followed Hugh along the corridor to the final large room in Home. She'd never ventured this far down the complex before and only knew it to be the farm because Hugh had told her so.

The closer they got to the end of the corridor, the thicker the air became with humidity; it reeked of hot damp soil. Vicky looked at the large door that shut the farm off from the rest of the complex. It seemed solid in both its construction and fit and clearly did a good job of containing the reek of the place.

When they reached the door, Hugh stopped and turned to look at Vicky. "I wanted to show you everywhere now that you're my deputy. We normally keep the farm separate from everyone. A rationed community doesn't need access to the place where all the food is made. And even if they could resist the chance to steal some food, the extra-strong UV bulbs would have the people flocking here. Did you wonder why Piotr was the most tanned Russian you'd ever seen?"

As Vicky thought back to her first impression of Piotr, she

laughed. He did have a surprisingly dark tan; it was like bored-housewife dark.

Hugh grabbed one side of the door with both hands. On runners, it slid across as Hugh dragged it with a grunt and revealed the third and final large room in Home.

Vicky's jaw dropped as she stepped forward. Similar in size to the vast canteen and kitchen area, the farm had the same high ceiling. Except, unlike the other spaces, every inch of the floor had been covered in damp earth. Now they'd stepped into the room, the heady reek of moist mud made the air harder to breathe.

Vicky's eyes widened as she took the room in; were the space outside, the size of it would have justified using machinery to work the land. But if they used anything like that inside, the exhaust fumes would make the air unbreathable.

Although one large carpet of wet earth, the ground had been separated into sections. Each had a crop of one sort or another growing in it, creating a patchwork effect. They even had a square of earth that looked like it had been left fallow.

Hugh leaned close to Vicky and said, "You can close your mouth now."

"This is amazing," Vicky said. "I've never seen anything like it in my life." Huge banks of lights hung from the ceiling. When Vicky looked up, she felt the UV rays sink into her skin.

"You can probably see why we need three hundred and twenty-seven solar panels now."

Vicky's mouth remained open and she nodded.

The large Piotr walked over to Hugh and Vicky. Dressed in just wellies and shorts, his semi-nakedness showed the body of someone used to hard graft. Heat smothered Vicky's face and she didn't know where to look.

A smile showed Vicky that he hadn't missed her reaction. Piotr then said in his thick Russian accent, "Welcome to my farm."

A glance across the room and Vicky saw a barn in one corner. "Is that where you keep the food?"

"Yes," Piotr said, "although, not so much food these past two years. Not a good harvest."

Worry lines painted deep grooves on Piotr's face as he stared down at Vicky, and when Vicky looked at Hugh, she saw the same taut anxiety gripped his features. Before she could push it any further, Hugh patted her back. "Right, there's more I need to show you. Thank you, Piotr."

"Welcome," the big man replied.

As Vicky followed Hugh back through the sliding door, she heard Piotr call out across the vast room to the seven or so workers busy in the fields. "Come on, you lazy *sobaki*. Work! Your life and your comrades lives depend on it." Although a booming call, the carpet of soil dampened his words.

Before Vicky could hear anymore of the chatter, Hugh slid the door back across and slammed it shut.

\*\*\*

Silence separated the pair as they walked up the next corridor. The smell of damp earth had been replaced with the familiar tang of bleach. Vicky finally said, "Piotr seemed worried about the harvest."

Hugh kept his eyes ahead as he spoke. "Yeah, he likes to be

overly cautious. In reality, we've been doing fine."

Hugh already seemed less worried than he had in the farm, but it could have been a front. He seemed keen to avoid the subject, so Vicky moved on and said, "So what did you do before this? You must have been, what, late twenties when everything went to shit."

Before Hugh could reply, Vicky said, "Let me guess."

With his back straight and his gaze still fixed ahead of them, Hugh marched down the corridor. It seemed so obvious now that Vicky thought about it. "You were military, right?"

A wry smile spread across Hugh's face. "I'm guessing at the age you must have been, you were on your way to being a sergeant or were already there?"

"I hadn't quite got there," Hugh said. "I didn't want the responsibility too early in my career. I just wanted to focus on being a grunt, you know?"

"So what did you do? Did you go on any tours?"

"A few. My main role was door-kicking in Mogadishu."

Too embarrassed to ask what he meant by that, Vicky nodded. "I knew it." Because she didn't know what else to say, she added, "You have military written all over you."

The comment seemed to inflate the man. If he didn't have military written all over him before then, he certainly did now as he marched into the kitchen area.

\*\*\*

After they'd crossed the kitchen and walked up the next corridor, they arrived at a locked room and Hugh pulled out a ring of keys. He looked both up and down the deserted corridor before he undid the lock with a snap and pulled the door wide.

A bank of monitors faced them, and Vicky gasped to see each one switched on, the collective glow of them lighting up the room.

After she'd followed Hugh in, he locked the door behind them.

"If you think about it hard enough, you can work out this room exists," Hugh said. "With the monitors in the canteen, it has to, right? In spite of that, I don't broadcast the fact. If everyone knew I had almost complete surveillance of the entire surrounding area, they'd never leave me alone."

"*Almost* complete surveillance?" Vicky asked.

"Yeah." Hugh walked over to a monitor that looked out over the field of solar panels. "We can't see all the way back here. If someone came at the solar panels from the far end, they could crawl beneath them and get all the way to our front door without detection."

"And there's no way to change that?"

"Not without losing a significant view somewhere else."

"You don't worry about someone sneaking up on you?"

"We invite people here, Vicky. The diseased are our only worry, and they don't creep anywhere. We'll see them, so it's not much of an issue."

As Hugh spoke, Vicky looked at all of the monitors and the view they afforded her. "You've got some proper escapism here, Hugh. If I were you, I'd spend a *lot* of time watching the outside world."

Hugh laughed. "I do."

Both of them watched the monitors as if searching for the

diseased outside. "I'm still pissed that so few people came out with us to fight," Hugh said. "We protect them, feed them, hell, we even do their fucking washing, but when we need them to fight, none of them seem interested. I'm trying to build an army here, and we have a group of lazy good-for-nothings. If even just ten percent of the community had come with us, that battle against the diseased would have been much easier."

A shrug of her shoulders and Vicky looked across to see the tension in Hugh's face. "I suppose some people aren't meant to fight. You should go a bit easier on them. Even the brave ones can lose courage on the battlefield."

The dig went straight over Hugh's head, his anger at the community seeming to dull his awareness. "But they're meant to eat, sleep, and wash here?"

"Look, I'm not saying it's right, but there has to be a more productive way to deal with it than getting aggressive."

A heavy sigh sank Hugh's entire frame and he looked down at his feet. "I'm sorry. I just get *so* frustrated. I feel like most of the people here are parasites. I have to deal with the day-to-day stresses of running this place, and they eat all our food and bring their petty little complaints to me when someone takes two fucking pieces of bread rather than one. It's like looking after children sometimes."

Although deadly serious, Vicky couldn't help but smile at Hugh and his rant. "So how about we try to do something to motivate them to contribute more?"

"Like what?"

"I dunno, enforced PT?"

"PT?"

"Physical training. Shouldn't you know that from your time in the army?"

"So how do we force them to work out?" Hugh said, ignoring Vicky's question.

Vicky paused for a moment and looked at the man. Had he been in the army? When she saw him awaiting a response, she said, "We make them all use the gym. We station someone on the door to verify they've been there. They have to get a certain amount of hours signed off every week. At least if we get them fit, they may feel more willing to go out and fight."

With his bottom lip in a pinch, Hugh nodded. "I see. That makes a lot of sense."

"We could get them all fit and then start forcing them outside every day on little chores. Even just twenty minutes at a time to get them used to the outside world. I'm guessing it would help you if other people stamped down the grass near the solar panels?"

Hugh smiled. "I knew asking for your help in running this place was a good idea. It seems so obvious now you say it, but I'd gotten so lost in my frustrations that I couldn't see a logical solution anymore."

All of the right words came from Hugh's mouth, but something in his dark eyes didn't connect with what he said. Before Vicky could challenge him, she saw movement on one of the monitors. "Look, three diseased."

The pair stared at the three figures. Something seemed different about them. None of them had the stooped gait of the diseased. Vicky drew a sharp breath. "I don't think they've been bitten."

The screens seemed large enough for it to be clear, but Hugh leaned closer anyway as he studied the three forms on the monitor. "Shit the bed," he said. "I think you're right."

# Chapter Thirteen

Vicky watched the people on the monitor with her mouth open wide. They stumbled a little, but they definitely didn't move like the diseased. She'd seen enough of the fuckers over the years to recognise the difference between human exhaustion and the infected.

Hugh broke the silence when he tugged on Vicky's arm and said, "Come on, we need to go and help them."

After they'd locked the monitor room behind them, they took off in the direction of the canteen. Hugh ran ahead and Vicky followed.

The sound of their heavy footfalls echoed in the tight corridor. As Hugh passed one of the closed doors, he banged on it, his hard whack booming through the tight space. "We need you, Jessica. New people have arrived."

Just before they entered the canteen, Vicky glanced behind to see Jessica burst from her room at a sprint. In her right hand she had a long and rusty machete.

The collective chatter in the canteen silenced the second they entered it, and everyone turned their way.

As if on cue, the people outside of Home came up on the monitors mounted on the far wall. It saved any need for explanation.

By the time they'd crossed the canteen and gotten close to the stairs that led up to the entranceway, Hugh had pointed at a young girl. Maybe slightly older than ten, she looked at him when he said, "You, come with us. We need someone on the door."

After they'd left the canteen, the people came to life again. Their excited chatter chased Vicky, Hugh, and Jessica up into Home's foyer.

A mixture of the run and the nervous anticipation of what lay ahead added rocket fuel to Vicky's pulse. When she stopped, every kick of her heart damn near rocked her where she stood. With her mouth spread wide, she tried to pull deep breaths into her body.

When Vicky looked out of one of the large windows, she saw the people as they stumbled toward Home. Hugh also watched them for a few seconds before he turned back to face Vicky and Jessica. "Okay, Vicky, what we do in this situation is go out and help the people. That's important." He pulled down three gas masks from a box mounted to the wall next to him. After he'd given one to Vicky and one to Jessica, he pulled the third one over his face. It muffled his words. "We don't really need these, but, as much as we want to help these people, it keeps them unsettled to see us like this. We don't know who these people are yet, and we need to keep control of the situation until we know they're all right."

The gas mask felt heavier than Vicky had expected, but she slipped it on all the same. A strange mix of halitosis and rubber ran through Vicky's sinuses and she screwed her face up against the funk of it. Although the mask had lenses and Vicky could see through them, they still clouded her view of the world around her. With her peripheral vision limited, she had to move her entire head to see.

"Right," Hugh said, "you guys ready for this?"

Vicky nodded. Maybe Jessica had too; Vicky couldn't tell with the mask on.

Hugh put his hand on the shoulder of the young girl they'd brought up with them and he leaned close to her. Quite an imposing sight, Hugh's appearance made the child recoil as she listened to his instructions. "Okay, you need to open this door for us and then lock it behind us once we're out."

The girl nodded.

"Then watch us through the window and open the door again when we come back and get close. Can you do that?"

The girl nodded again.

"Good," Hugh said and shoved a chair over to her with his foot.

Nausea flipped in Vicky's guts as she watched the girl stand on the chair. After the second heavy crack, she opened the door to let them outside.

Obviously used to this, Hugh and Jessica stepped out without hesitation. And maybe they didn't see it in Vicky, but reluctance tugged on her frame as she followed them. After she'd been so judgmental of Hugh when Serj fell over, maybe she should have been bolder in leaving Home. Jessica slipped her long machete into a sheath she wore on her back. Neither Vicky nor Hugh had a weapon on them. Hopefully they wouldn't need them.

Without another word, Hugh set off at a jog toward the three people. Vicky and Jessica followed.

Not the first time Vicky had been outside of the community, but she hadn't worn a gas mask before. Sure, it made them look as freaky as hell, but it seemed like a large compromise considering the loss of peripheral vision. The uneven ground also presented more of a challenge, the large snout blocking her line of sight, so she wouldn't notice the potholes and undulations as they ran.

Two men and a woman, the three new people stopped and raised their hands as if they'd had a gun pointed at them. They looked dirty, unshaven, and exhausted. God knew where they'd come from.

All three of them watched Hugh through wide eyes in their dirty faces.

"Welcome to Home," he said. "If you come here with peace in your heart, know that we will always have space for you."

None of the three spoke.

Jessica stepped forward. "Hi, guys, let us take you inside so we can get you cleaned up and rested, okay?"

The woman seemed more distressed than the others as she stared at Jessica and shivered. She looked to be in her forties. She had wild matted hair and pale skin.

"Okay?" Jessica repeated.

The woman nodded and her entire body shook.

The sound of the heavy wind pulled Vicky's attention away and she spun on the spot to take in her surroundings. At least she had her hearing should any of the diseased approach. It seemed clear.

After Jessica and Hugh had grabbed someone each, Vicky took the arm of the last man and they all headed back toward Home at a gentle jog.

Although Vicky pulled on the man, he tugged against her, tired reluctance in his heavy frame. The ground, uneven beneath her feet, the long grass whipping her legs, and now the man who couldn't run any quicker than a jog, all put Vicky on edge. They just needed a herd of diseased to complete the picture.

The crack of the two bolts snapped through the air when they got close to Home, and the small girl opened the door, a grim set to her small face as she pulled it wider.

First Jessica and Hugh ran in with their charges, and then Vicky followed behind with the slow man.

The second they stepped inside, Vicky pulled her mask away and breathed the fresher air. Her skin had turned damp with sweat, and it now cooled down as the moisture evaporated from her face.

The three newest arrivals looked bewildered as they stared from Hugh to Vicky then to Jessica, and none of them spoke. The woman in the group continued to shake and shiver as she drew stuttered breaths through her clenched teeth. A sheen of sweat covered her pale skin. She reminded Vicky of an addict going through withdrawal.

After Hugh had put the three gas masks away, he offered his hand to the group one at a time. "Hi, I'm Hugh. Welcome to Home."

Although clearly shocked, the slightest moment of hope lifted the faces of all three of the new arrivals. They didn't seem to want to allow themselves the relief at that moment. And living in the world they did, why should they? Things went wrong in this life. Things went wrong pretty fucking quickly.

After Jessica had shaken their hands, Vicky did the same. She got to the woman last, and as Vicky held her hand, she froze. When she looked into the woman's fearful eyes, she saw it. Suddenly the woman's state made sense.

Dropping the woman's hand like she would a hot coal, Vicky stepped back from her. "She's been bitten."

A ring of steel sounded out as Jessica drew her machete, raised it above her head, and glared at the woman.

The woman shook her head. "No, no, it's … it's just a cut, honestly."

The ice queen that Vicky had met when she first came to home resurfaced in Jessica, who kept a hold of her blade and remained fixed on the woman. "Show me."

Grief buckled the woman's face and her eyes filled with tears. Hysteria gripped a hold of her and she grabbed her forearm. "I've *not* been bitten."

The two men by her side glanced at one another.

When she picked up on this, the woman shook her head some more. "Please, it's only a cut. I've not been bitten."

The woman looked at Jessica as if to appeal to her softer side. Ice stared back at her and Jessica said in a low growl, "Show me your fucking arm."

A shake, more violent than before, ran through the woman as she pulled her sleeve back. A deep gash sat in her pale skin that belched dark red blood. So clearly a bite, Vicky saw the individual teeth marks in the wound.

Silence swept through the entranceway. The two men

watched with their eyes on stalks. Jessica cocked an eyebrow at the woman. The woman stopped shaking, frozen in her fear.

As cold as her glare, Jessica stepped closer to the woman and said, "We can't let you put this community in danger."

Vicky might have had most of her attention on the woman and her pale fear, but she didn't miss Hugh pull the small girl toward him. After a quick word in her ear, he gently nudged her away and she ran down the stairs into the canteen. She didn't need to see this.

# Chapter Fourteen

The silence seemed to last an age as Vicky watched Jessica stare down at the scruffy and infected woman. The woman recoiled from Jessica, who continued to hold her machete aloft, tense and ready to use it.

The pound of Vicky's heart beat so heavily it damn near rocked her where she stood.

The gentle footsteps of Serj broke through the moment as he limped up the stairs and over to the front door of Home. As if in support of his love's tough choice, he pulled the first lock free with a snap before he leaned down—wincing from the clear discomfort in his ankle—and released the second. Both loud cracks called out as a judge's gavel would when condemning a criminal. No quarter would be given.

When Serj pulled the door wide, the strong wind rushed into the place and stirred up the muddy smell of dirt on the three newest arrivals. The chill ran goosebumps along Vicky's arms, and her entire frame tensed against the need to shiver. A glance across at both men and she realised that she too stood as stunned as them, wide-eyed and with her mouth hanging open.

When Jessica pointed her machete at the open door, the woman shook her head. Her messy hair waved with the motion, and her frantic words spilled from her mouth. "No, no, no. Please, don't do this. Please, I'm okay, honestly. It's nothing, I'll be *fine* ..." Her last word trailed off into sobs.

But Jessica didn't back down. Instead, she continued to glare at the woman and pointed her machete in the direction of the open door again.

The woman drew a deep breath, but before she could protest again, Jessica darted forward.

The movement made Vicky jump and she let out a startled yelp.

In one swift movement, Jessica grabbed the woman's skinny arm and threw her at the door.

The woman's clumsy footsteps played a beat against the floor and she nearly fell. Hunched by the entranceway to Home like a scolded dog that wouldn't leave, no matter how many times it got beaten, the woman cried freely. Tears mixed with snot as they streaked her dirty face. Her mouth bent out of shape. "We've fought so hard to get here. Twelve of us set out and only three of us have survived."

"Two," Hugh said, his tone cold as he moved next to Jessica and looked at the woman, his arms folded across his chest.

For the briefest moment, the woman looked from Jessica to Hugh and back to Jessica before she broke down again.

Jessica sighed. The sound probably sounded like impatience to the two men who didn't know Jessica well, but Vicky—who didn't know her much better—recognised it as regret. Jessica shoved the woman again, so she ended up outside of Home.

Once Jessica had followed the woman outside, one of the men—the short squat one, his hair and beard both long and dirty—turned to Hugh. "Come on, man, surely there must be another way?"

Disgust wiped a sneer across Hugh's face. "Are you *new* or something?" he asked. "Or maybe you know something I don't? Please, tell me how you've managed to cure people who have been bitten before?"

A slight pause and the man said, "What if it's not a bite?"

Because she'd seen it more clearly than Hugh had, Vicky stepped forward. As a guard for Home, they needed to be united on this. "Her wound has *teeth* marks in it. How can that *not* be a bite?"

When the man turned to Vicky, a darkness stirred behind his eyes that forced Vicky back a couple of paces. Something about his silent glare held a threat to all of their safety.

"Look," Hugh said, "drop the attitude, yeah? We're prepared to take you two in, feed you, look after you, *and* help nurse you back to full strength. So a little gratitude would be nice. Also, we're just about to put your travelling companion out of her misery so you don't have to. Unless you want to go out there with her and watch her turn into one of those things, then I suggest you shut the fuck up." With a tiny gap between his thumb and forefinger, Hugh held it up at the man. "I'm this close to turning you two away, just so you know."

The man dropped his head and shoulders with a weighted sigh and focused on the ground. His friend—the taller one of the two, who also had the same dirty look to his blond and dishevelled hair—also kept quiet. But he didn't look down.

Instead, he looked from the bitten woman to Jessica. His eyes were bloodshot like those of an alcoholic.

A flash of movement outside pulled Vicky's attention from the two men to Jessica. The woman had run back at the entranceway to Home, and Jessica shoved her away with such force, the woman stumbled and landed on her arse. Grief twisted the woman's lank features as she remained on the ground and stared up.

When she moved to get up again, Jessica raised a hand at her. "Stay there." What she said next turned Vicky's blood to ice. "It'll be easier on both of us."

The woman looked like she still intended to stand up.

"I'm being serious. Your time's up and you need to accept that. I know life hasn't been easy since the disease, but no one can help you now."

A feral scream and the woman jumped to her feet and ran at Jessica again.

This time, Jessica stepped forward with her machete and yelled back. She brought the old rusty weapon over in a wide arc. The woman raised her arm to block it, but flesh had little to offer against the force of the sharp blade.

A wet squelch as the weapon cut a deep gash in the woman's arm, and the crazed woman screamed again and fell away. As she rolled on the ground, Jessica closed in on her, shutting her down.

The woman lifted her hand up at Jessica, the fresh wound on her arm gushing blood.

With her jaw clenched, Jessica drove another heavy blow against the cowering woman. This time the blade buried in the woman's raised palm and split her hand in two. A heave lifted through Vicky and she looked away. Maybe she imagined it, but at that moment she could smell the metallic reek of spilled blood.

Only able to listen to the rest of the fight, Vicky heard Jessica grunt before the squelch of the blade as it embedded in the woman again. The woman's scream came out as shrill and ear-splitting. When Vicky glanced back up, her mind struggled to see the scene in front of her clearly, her thoughts scrambled because of the sheer amount of spilled blood.

While it happened, it seemed to last a lifetime. And then it ended. The crazed woman lay still on the ground, red and glistening in her own blood. Her sunken eyes sat wide on her gaunt face. Jessica stood over her and gasped for breath, remorse hanging from her features.

Both of the men who'd arrived with the recently executed woman stared out of the window at their dead friend. When Hugh grabbed the arm of one of them—the taller and slimmer of the two—the man pulled it away.

"Have you changed your mind?" Hugh said to him, clearly wound up from the brutal execution he'd just witnessed. "Do you want to leave? Because I'm starting to think that might be for the best."

The fight visibly left the man and he allowed Hugh to drag him away. Serj grabbed the other man, who continued to look over his shoulder as they walked off. Despite Serj's limp, the man didn't fight him, but he did say, "I'm not going to let her get away with that."

A hard shove from Serj and the man stumbled forward.

Normally calm, Serj stared at him, his teeth clenched as fury burned in his dark eyes. "If I hear you speak about my partner once more, I will personally *gut* you. You got that?"

Instead of a reply, the man followed his friend and Hugh down the stairs toward the canteen.

When Hugh called back to Vicky, his voice echoed in the tunnelled stairs. "Go out and help Jessica with the body, please. She may have brought the disease to our door, but the woman deserves to be buried."

## Chapter Fifteen

The dead woman had been so covered in her own blood that Vicky couldn't avoid getting it on her as she helped Jessica carry the corpse up the small hill that led to the back of Home. If she hadn't smelled the metallic reek of spilled claret before, it damn near clogged her nostrils now; the fierce wind was no match for the stench of death.

When they reached the top, Vicky's chest tight from the effort, she looked at Jessica; the woman seemed as calm as she always did, her tight ponytail holding fast against the strong breeze. The ice queen took on an entirely different meaning now. Jessica would do things the others couldn't. "So where do we bury her?"

After she'd scoffed at her, Jessica said, "You don't believe that we actually bury people, do you? You poor woman. We don't bury anyone here."

"You don't?"

"Why would we? Especially with the racket that woman made. I guarantee you that any diseased within a five-mile radius heard her screams, and they're heading toward us right now. I don't know about you, but I ain't prepared to risk my life for *her*."

With the weight of the woman still pulling on her arms, Vicky shifted to get more comfortable, the blood on her hands making it hard to keep a tight grip on the corpse. A snap of her head to the side to flick her hair from her face and she said, "So where do we put her?"

Jessica led them a short distance along the ridge.

When Vicky saw a collection of bodies, she baulked. "What the hell?"

"People die, Vicky, and we need to put the bodies somewhere."

"And all of the people they left behind believe they were buried out here?"

"Yep."

Flies flew around the pile of corpses, each body at a different stage of decomposition. Maggots crawled over them in a writhing mass of white. The continual pulpy movement somehow animated the inanimate.

"Why didn't you just lock the woman out and sound the alarm?" Vicky said.

"Because sometimes we don't need to make a big song and dance about killing people. It's not good for morale. It's different when someone loses the plot inside of Home. That's a risk to our safety, if nothing else, and it comforts those on the right side of sanity that we can't tolerate such instability. But this woman came to us for help and we buried a machete in her."

Vicky admired the fact that Jessica got shit done, but maybe she took her cold detachment too far. As Vicky continued to look at the rotting remains, she shook her head. "I still think we should bury her."

"And who's going to dig the hole? Do you know how long that'll take?" A shrug and Jessica looked away from Vicky as if to survey the land around Home. "I'm happy to leave you here, but I need you to make a decision now because I'm not going to wait around while you get all emotional."

The words stung and Vicky clenched her jaw so she didn't tell Jessica to go fuck herself; it wouldn't get them anywhere and would only validate Jessica's assessment of her.

With her attention back on Vicky, Jessica said, "So you want me to leave you here, do you?"

Vicky shook her head.

"Right then,"—Jessica swung the corpse—"we need to launch her. Three … two … one …" On one they let go of the woman and Vicky watched her fly through the air, her limbs limp from death and yet to suffer the effects of rigour mortis.

Before she'd landed with a wet *thump,* Jessica had turned her back on the dead woman and headed back down toward Home's entrance. "Come on, Vicky," she called over her shoulder. "Let's get the fuck out of here and get cleaned up."

What could Vicky do? She could hardly give the woman a ceremony. A few more seconds passed, during which time Vicky stared at the dead and bloody corpse before she chased off down the hill after Jessica. She had to care less if she were to help run the community. Hard decisions had to be made from time to time, and she couldn't always expect Jessica to make them.

# Chapter Sixteen

There might have been a two-hour window for breakfast, but when Flynn and Vicky arrived with half an hour to go, it seemed like most of the community had the same idea. Like when Vicky used to stay in cheap hotels with a similar policy, the last thirty minutes saw the place fill up with bleary-eyed guests as they munched on sausages—which seemed to be filled with anything but pork—and hash browns.

As Vicky spooned another mouthful of the plain wheat cereal into her mouth, she screwed her face up at the stale flavour of the powdered milk. Maybe the people in Home had acquired the taste for it, but for Vicky, her stomach responded to every swallow with the beginning of a heave. More watery than before from what must have been a thinning of their supplies, she munched the cereal without enthusiasm and sighed.

"What's up?" Flynn said.

A cow chewing the cud, Vicky shrugged. "I'd kill for sausages and hash browns right about now. Even the cheap shit they used to serve in the crappy motorway hotels."

A smile lit up Flynn's face and his eyes sparkled. "Me too."

But Vicky didn't smile in return. Dressed in the khaki uniform of the Home guards, she looked around the room at the people gathered there. What would they think had they seen the way Jessica dealt with the infected woman? It took for Vicky to witness it to realise that tough decisions needed to be made by those in power. Maybe she'd been naive to think it would be any other way.

For the second time in as many minutes, Flynn said, "What's up?"

Of everyone in the place, she wanted to protect Flynn the most. As he adjusted to a life in Home, he didn't need to know all of its dark secrets. "Nothing, why?"

"You seem distant. Like you have something on your mind."

It almost ached to smile, but Vicky forced one anyway.

Flynn pulled back at what must have been a ghastly sight. He frowned at her. "You can tell me, you know."

Maybe she could. After all, she'd shut him out for long enough, so maybe she should treat him like the adult he was and confide in him. If Rhys were there at that moment, she would have shared her worries with him. A nod and Vicky drew her breath to reply, but before she could say anything, Hugh appeared at their table and sat down beside Flynn.

Hugh looked pissed. Vicky's turn to say, "Are you okay?"

Although Hugh gave her a sharp nod, he scanned the large canteen area as if paranoid about listening ears, but no one seemed interested in them. The collective sound of chatter swirled in the ceiling space above them. A room full of people without a care in the world because of Hugh and his team.

"Come on, Hugh, I can tell something's up." When she

looked at Flynn, he raised his eyebrows at her as if to highlight the fact that he'd just been asking her the same thing. Vicky ignored him and turned to Hugh again. "What's going on?"

As Hugh released a heavy sigh, he dragged his hand over the top of his head, pulling his hair from his eyes. "You know what we spoke about with the gym time?"

Vicky nodded.

"Well, I want to address that now. I need to tell the people here that we need more from them."

With his hand still on the top of his head, Hugh continued to scan the room with his dark eyes.

Another mouthful of the watery and sweet cereal and Vicky looked at Flynn. "Many of the people here don't pull their weight. We think they should exercise more so they'll feel confident to go outside when we need it. Although, we don't want to reveal that part of the plan to them yet. Phase one is to get them fit. After that, we can hopefully start taking the fight to the diseased."

When Hugh stood up, his chair screeched out behind him. So consumed with their own conversations, very few people seemed to notice his actions.

Vicky hadn't seen the red plastic whistle on a string around his neck until Hugh lifted it to his mouth and wrapped his lips around it. In anticipation of the shrill sound, Vicky winced. A second later, a prolonged and sharp *peep* called through the vast open room and cannoned around in the ceiling space above.

The way every face snapped to attention and stared at Hugh took Vicky back through the countless times a horde of diseased had noticed her. The hive mind focused on the leader of Home and silence swept through the room like a strong gust.

Now that he had their attention, Hugh stood up on his chair. "It seems like most of you are here, which is good. For the people who aren't, I want you to relay my message to them."

Each face stared at Hugh as they let him speak.

"Home is a hard place to run and we're lucky that we now have a new person to help with that." A slight pause and Hugh looked down at Vicky. "But it's not enough. We've existed for the longest time, but we need to grow as a community into something much better than what we currently are."

For a few seconds, Hugh didn't speak and simply took in all the faces that stared at him. "Phase one is to make sure everyone's fit. Unless you have a legitimate health condition, we expect you to log ten hours' gym time per week. I'm not saying you all need to be super athletes, but we can *all* get fitter. Become the fittest person you can be and I'll be happy. We're going to place someone on the door of the gym and they'll stamp you in and out to log the times you've spent exercising. I'll be checking the cards every week."

A Middle Eastern-looking man got to his feet and called across the vast space, "And what if we don't do it?"

Hugh massaged his temples and drew a deep breath. Vicky could see that for the longest time, he'd let his frustrations with the people of Home bubble beneath the surface. Because he hadn't addressed it, he now seemed to struggle with holding his rage back.

Vicky stood up and felt the attention of the room shift to her. It threw her off momentarily, heat smothered her, and she pulled at her collar as if it would help her breathe more easily.

"We all have to do things we don't like. I had to go outside and fight the diseased because none of you lot would. After ten years of doing that, do you think I really want to do it some more?"

Silence.

"Well, I don't. But I do it because we all need to be accountable. We need to help Home survive. What will you lot do if the few of us who go outside get killed? Who will have the courage to run this place then? We can all get fitter, stronger, and more adept at coping with life as it currently is. The diseased aren't going anywhere, so we need to learn to continue to survive with them still around."

Some of the crowd nodded at Vicky.

After Vicky sat down, Hugh winked at her before he turned to the room again. "To be a part of any society, you have to contribute. Home has been a free ride for too long and that needs to change. If you don't want to take part, just say." Although he'd addressed the room until that point, he focused on the Middle Eastern man when he said, "We can open the front door for anyone."

Enough people gasped at Hugh's threat for it to cut through the large space, and Hugh scanned the place for a few more seconds before he nodded to himself and sat down again.

For the next few minutes, Hugh said nothing. At any one time, it seemed like about a third of the room watched him as if he would offer an alternative to them getting off their lazy arses.

When the stares finally died down, Hugh looked at Flynn. "I have a job for you, mate."

Pride straightened Flynn's back and he smiled at Hugh.

"I want you to monitor the comings and goings at the gym.

I want you to stamp people in and out. We have an abundance of notebooks, so we'll use them for everyone, and we have a stamp that bites a hole in the paper."

"Why me? Why can't someone else do it?"

"Because you've not been here long and you seem like a stand-up guy. You're much less likely to be coerced into stamping people's books who don't exercise. Although, when we explain that phase two is going outside of Home, maybe that'll be enough motivation for them to do it anyway."

Flynn glared at Vicky. Maybe he knew she wouldn't let him go out and fight, or maybe he simply guessed as much. Either way, he clearly blamed her for his new role in Home.

Hugh stood up again and patted Flynn on the back. "You're a good lad, Flynn. I've set up a pile of books and a stamp outside the gym already. Once you've finished your breakfast, if you could go over there and get prepared for the first people, that would be great." Hugh turned his attention on Vicky. "Come on, we need to go."

Several quick spoonfuls filled Vicky's mouth with the flat taste of watery milk and wheat biscuits. She got to her feet in the glare of Flynn's rage, winced at him, and mouthed the word *sorry* before she followed Hugh out of the canteen.

In truth, she didn't feel very sorry. Flynn would be safe in Home and he'd be doing something useful, so Hugh would be likely to keep him there. Even now, after she'd seen him fight as well as his father had, Vicky couldn't let Flynn outside of Home. She loved him too much to let him die.

# Chapter Seventeen

The two corridors that ran between the canteen and the kitchen area seemed virtually identical. Each one had doors along either side with a small room behind them. Both sides were used purely for accommodation. Most of the doors—all of them painted white and with the same plain silver door handles on—remained closed. The only ones that still hung open were the ones currently unoccupied. The smell of bleach hung heavy in the air. Vicky could get used to most smells, but for some reason, the reek of bleach never felt any less abusive to her senses.

"We could find a separate room for Flynn now, if you like."

As Vicky kept stride with Hugh, she tried to see the subtext in his statement. If he had one, he'd hidden it well. He walked with his eyes focused on where they headed and with his chin raised. With everything that had happened in her life up until this point, Vicky didn't feel ready to trust him yet. Brendan had convinced her to lower her guard and she'd paid dearly for that—the entire bloody country had paid dearly for that … maybe more if it had reached those beyond the waters surrounding the UK.

"I'm not sure he's ready for that," Vicky said.

"Not sure if *he's* ready, or not sure if *you're* ready?"

"It doesn't matter if I'm ready or not. He lost his parents just a few short weeks ago. He'll need some more time to adjust to things, and I'll be there for him for as long as it takes." She steered the conversation away from talk of Flynn's accommodation. "Thanks for giving him the gym job, by the way."

"Huh?"

"Look, you and I both know the boy can fight better than most of the people in this place, but if he works in the gym, it means he has much less time to get outside of Home and put himself in danger. You giving him that job has ensured his safety."

A click of his fingers and Hugh smiled. "That wasn't my intention, but that makes sense now. I did wonder why he looked so pissed off. I like that kid; he's got spirit."

"That he has." With her steps falling into line with Hugh's, Vicky smiled. "That he has."

\*\*\*

As one, Vicky and Hugh stepped out into the huge kitchen area. The stainless steel workspace for the chefs would have looked large in most places, but in the corner of the cavernous room it seemed tiny. The medic bay—a small bed and very few supplies—looked as neglected as it always did. "Do you even use that bed anymore?"

Hugh said nothing for a few seconds as he stared at the rickety bed in the corner as if he'd seen too many people die on it already. He then shook his head. "No. It had more use back in the day when we had some medical supplies. Now people are better off in their room than lying out here in the open."

"Then why don't you get rid of it?"

"Quite a statement, wouldn't you say? Get rid of the medic bay and we publicly admit what we privately know; if you get injured, you're fucked."

Before Vicky could reply, Jessica emerged from the corridor that ran parallel with the one Vicky and Hugh had walked down. She had a pole slung over her shoulder and a collection of dead animals hung from it.

They arrived at the kitchen area at the same time, the smell of boiled vegetables in the air, but Hugh and Vicky stood back as Jessica laid the large stick down on the side with a heaving sigh. "Three rabbits, two foxes, seven squirrels, and a cat."

The chef—a fat and sweaty woman with angry red skin and heavy bags beneath her eyes—nodded at Jessica. "Thank you. We can put all of these to good use."

After she'd received the chef's approval, Jessica turned to Vicky and Hugh. "Everything okay?"

Hugh shrugged. "Okay. I told the people today that I expected them to exercise more."

"Oh?"

"Yeah, I'm not sure it went down too well, but they took it at least. Phase one is under way."

A knowing nod and Jessica turned to Vicky. "How are you?"

For some reason, the attention from the once hostile woman warmed Vicky and she felt herself grow inside by a few inches. "I'm fine, thank you. Are you okay? And Serj?"

Jessica's already friendly demeanour opened up into a broad smile. "We're both great, thank you. Serj's ankle aches a little now, but he should be back to full action very soon."

Vicky returned a smile before Jessica spun on her heel and walked away. As Vicky watched her back, a sway to her hips, her trousers a tight fit around her toned butt, and her blonde hair scraped back in the perfect ponytail, she saw beauty where she had once seen coldness. The woman stood as a vision of power and radiance. No wonder Vicky had found her so intimidating at the beginning.

"Can we get some food for our two newest arrivals, please, Fran?"

The large chef nodded at Hugh and plated up two bowls of stew. She then placed them both on one tray and slid it toward him.

"Thanks, sweetheart."

The slightest hint of a smile lifted the sides of Fran's mouth. And why wouldn't it? Vicky even found herself charmed by Hugh's charisma. It helped that he stood as tall and strong as he did. A winning smile and always prepared to dish out a compliment, he could probably have the pick of any woman in the place.

Vicky followed Hugh out of the kitchen area and nodded at Fran as she passed her. The smile fell from Fran's face as if the scaffolding holding it up had collapsed.

As they neared the next corridor, similar in layout to the one that separated the kitchen and canteen, Vicky said, "So Jessica does all of the hunting for Home?"

"Yep. She's the best we've got."

As much as Vicky didn't want to appear egotistical about hunting, and even though she wanted to feel comfortable with Jessica's clear strength and beauty, she said it anyway. "I'm good at hunting. You should let me try."

Hugh didn't reply.

\*\*\*

The corridor with the gym on it and the cells with their two newest citizens looked different from the other corridor because many of the rooms existed without doors. Storage areas, empty spaces, and the gym ... none of them needed to be closed off.

With their close proximity to the two men in their cells, Vicky moved nearer to Hugh and spoke so hopefully only he would hear it. "Will you keep the newest arrivals in their cells for longer than two days?"

Dropping his pace, Hugh shrugged. "Dunno. I'm a little worried about how they were with Jessica. I won't let them out if I think they're a danger to anyone here."

"I agree. I think you have to be careful with those two."

The two newest guests might not have had windows in their cell doors, but, unlike Flynn's cell, they did have small holes in the bottom for Hugh to slip their food through. When they got to the first one, Hugh crouched down, opened the hatch with a loud *snap,* and pushed the bowl of stew in. "Get it while it's hot."

They had the next man locked up a few doors down. Enough of a distance separated the two so they couldn't talk to one another should they want to. Hugh repeated the process as he slid the second bowl of stew through the gap.

Once he'd snapped the second hatch shut, Hugh placed the empty tray on the floor outside the cell. "Remind me to take the tray back later. I think we should go and check in the gym. I want to see—"

Before he could finish his sentence, raised voices ran up the corridor from the farm at the end of it. Without another word, Hugh took off toward the noise at a sprint and Vicky followed closely behind.

The hammer of their feet rattled through the hard confined space as Vicky and Hugh ran down it. The shouts at the far end continued; it was a clear conflict between two men.

When Hugh got to the end, he slid the door aside and ran into the humid and earthy room. Piotr stood by the door and watched the two men square off against one another. Some of the larger people in Home worked in the farm because it was the most physically demanding job. As Vicky looked at the two men in dirty grey tracksuits, she gasped at their size.

"Have you seen it?" the more irate of the two men said. Slightly smaller than the other man, his dark brown skin glistened with sweat in the humid room.

The other man sighed. "What do you want me to do about it?"

"We need to tell them; it's the only thing we can do."

The more defensive of the two men turned to Piotr at that point and raised his eyebrows. Piotr shrugged.

"I said," the first man snarled, "we need to tell people. They have a right to know."

In a flash, Hugh darted forward, and before the angry man could look up, he drove a right cross into his chin. The dark-skinned man's eyes rolled back in his head and his legs folded beneath him. He hit the wet soil with a thud.

The man he'd been arguing with stared down at his fallen opponent and shook his head. When he looked at Hugh, he said, "I didn't know what to do with him."

Hugh's reply snapped back at him like a cracking whip. "Try what I just did. We can't have hysteria in this place. Now take him to one of the holding cells." Hugh turned to look at the large Russian. "Piotr, can you please help him?"

Near silence surrounded the group for a few minutes as the two farm workers lifted their unconscious colleague and carried him out through the still open door.

Once they'd gone, Vicky turned to the clearly agitated Hugh. "Well?"

"Well what?" Hugh said.

"What was all that about?"

"I dunno. As you've seen, this place drives people crazy. Some time in a cell should sort him out."

But Vicky could see Hugh had a lot more information on the conflict that he hadn't told her. The man clearly wanted to tell the people of Home something. However, Hugh didn't seem keen on sharing what that something was with Vicky.

Before she could push the matter any further, Hugh said, "Why don't you go back to your room for a while? Take an early lunch and we'll meet up later in the gym, yeah?" And with that, Hugh walked past Vicky and left her in the farm area on her own.

# Chapter Eighteen

After she'd had lunch, Vicky walked the long corridor to the gym. The usual smell of bleach damn near made her eyes water. One of the locked doors had the man from the farm behind it. As tempting as it was to find out which one and talk to him, Vicky kept on walking. She didn't need Hugh catching her with the man. If she wanted to know what the fight was about, she'd have to get it from Hugh.

When Vicky got close enough to the gym, she finally looked at Flynn, who sat outside it at a desk. "How are you getting on?"

"How do you think I'm getting on?"

Of course the boy would be pissed. Sat on a hard plastic chair at a tiny desk with a stamp and a smile seemed a long way away from going outside of Home and defending the place against the diseased. But as long as he stayed there he'd be safe, so Vicky could tolerate his bad attitude. From the way he sat, coiled as if ready to launch himself at her, Vicky didn't continue the conversation and walked straight past him into the gym.

As a parting gesture, Flynn called in after her, "You need to get a stamp."

The slightest smile lifted on Vicky's face at his teenage petulance, but she played the game, removed her mirth, and went back to his small table. "Can I get a book too, please?"

Flynn didn't look at her when he picked a book up, stamped it with the smiley face that pierced the page, and slid it along the table to her.

"Thank you." And with that, Vicky entered the gym again.

The usual stale smell of damp and sweat mixed as a heady musk in the air of the small room. Vicky headed straight for the treadmill, threw her sweatshirt down on the floor, and set it to number seven so she could warm up with a fast walk.

As the only person in the gym, Vicky shook her head. Despite Hugh's impassioned speech about working out, the people of Home didn't seem to have taken him seriously.

Each step warmed Vicky up a little more than the last. Her heart beat harder from the exercise. Even walking gave her a workout, but she soon upped the speed on the treadmill until she'd found her thumping rhythm. Despite running at number eleven whenever she ran next to Hugh, Vicky found the comfort to keep going at around ten, so she set it there and lifted her head to watch the entranceway to the gym.

Only about five minutes passed before Vicky heard raised voices come down the corridor toward her. It sounded like Hugh and Jessica, although with the sound of the treadmill's belt and the slam of her feet against it, Vicky couldn't hear what they said to one another; stopping would make it too obvious.

Hugh walked in a few seconds later, and Jessica continued past the room, her jawline tense and a scowl on her face. Hugh said nothing to Flynn as he marched into the place. He stepped onto the treadmill, his usual light-heartedness absent from his demeanour. Without a word, he set it straight to number eleven.

Within a minute, Hugh had locked into his fast run. Maybe Vicky imagined it, but his feet seemed to slam down harder than usual with each step, almost as if he stamped his frustration on the treadmill's belt.

Since their fight outside of Home with the diseased, Vicky had seen a different side to Hugh. It seemed like things were going wrong for him. Most of the people did nothing to help, and there had been infighting in the farm. Although, there had to be more to that one. Whatever the farm worker had wanted to say, Hugh had made sure he couldn't. Not that Vicky could ask him about it at that point—hell, she didn't even want to look at the guy in his current frame of mind. The beeps of her treadmill called out as she eased it up to eleven and fell into stride next to him.

Hugh's aggression thickened the muggy air in the gym. For a moment, Vicky felt inclined to stop her treadmill and get off. But why should she? If she and Hugh were to run this place together, she couldn't be bullied into silence. Whatever issues he had, he had to learn to deal with them more productively.

"So what was that about with Jessica?" Vicky asked.

A snap of his head to face her and Hugh scowled at Vicky.

Vicky returned his stare with interest. "Well?"

As the leader of Home, Hugh clearly didn't get challenged often; he said nothing for a few seconds, his feet slamming down even harder. It could have gone one of two ways. Fortunately, Hugh snapped out of his mood. "We were trying to sort a few things out."

Vague, but at least he said something. "Sort things out?"

"Sorry," Hugh said and shook his head. "I've been a little distracted lately. I'm finding it hard to deal with the fact that we have so many freeloaders in this place, and when I ask them to start working out to get fit, they clearly ignore me." Gassed from his run, Hugh turned the setting down on his treadmill and slowed to a fast walk. "Sometimes I wonder why I take on all the stress when very few people seem willing to share it with me. They get fat on our food, they wash with our hot water, they read by the light of our electricity, yet when I ask for something from them, they ignore me."

Before Vicky could reply, Hugh said, "You know what?" He cracked his hand against the large red button on the treadmill so hard it shook the entire machine. "I'm not taking this bullshit."

Red-faced and glistening with sweat, Hugh picked his top up from the ground.

"What are you doing?" Vicky asked.

"I'm going to talk to them. I'm not being the mug of this place any longer."

As Hugh walked out of the gym, Vicky jumped off the treadmill and picked up her sweatshirt before she followed him out. Although Flynn glared at her again, she returned her attention to Hugh and jogged off up the corridor after him.

\*\*\*

They'd travelled from the gym to the canteen in silence. With his fists clenched and his jaw set tight, Hugh focused straight ahead and marched like he wanted to kill someone.

When they stepped from the tight corridor into the open space of the canteen, Vicky ran her eyes over the vast space. At least half of Home sat about chatting or watching the kids play.

"Right," Hugh shouted, his loud voice echoing through the place like a P.E. teacher in a sports hall. "I don't know what the fuck you think this place is, but whatever your perceptions are, they need to fucking change." Some of the adults pulled children away or covered their ears, but if Hugh noticed it, he didn't care. "We need more help, which means you lot need to get fitter. Even if you don't get fit, you're going to start pulling your weight anyway. Everyone's had a free ride in this place for far too long." Hugh stepped aside and pointed at Vicky. "She's been here less than a week and she's done more than most of you lazy shits have in the entire time you've been here. And some of you have been here for a fucking *decade*."

Heat flushed Vicky's cheeks and panic tightened her chest to have the entire canteen stare at her. She dropped her attention to the floor and rocked on the balls of her feet.

"Now the gym's too small to accommodate all of you lazy fucks at the same time, so you, you, and you," Hugh said as he pointed to two women and a man—they seemed to be the three largest people in the room. "Get down there now and do an hour each. I expect to see your stamped books by the end of today."

A few eyes rolled and mouths hung open in shock, but nobody questioned Hugh's order as they stood up, lethargic in their actions.

Quiet consumed the canteen as everyone continued to watch Hugh, and Hugh stared at the three people he'd ordered to exercise. Their slow movements wound the tension tighter as they shuffled from their seats past the leader of Home. The first two left the room with their eyes lowered. The third one, a blonde woman with blotchy skin, drew a breath to speak when she got level with Hugh.

Before she could get her words out, Hugh said, "I don't care what you have to say. If you can walk, you can exercise. Get your fat arse down to the gym now."

After they'd gone, Hugh turned to Vicky and spoke loud enough so everyone could hear. "Lazy fucks. If I have to wedge a rocket up their arses permanently, then that's what I'll fucking do. I ain't taking it any more. I've had enough."

Vicky opened her mouth to respond, but Hugh spun on his heel before she had the chance, and walked off. He called over his shoulder as he disappeared down the same corridor the people he'd sentenced to exercise had, "Meet me tomorrow morning by the front door. Just after breakfast. We don't need to do anything else today."

Left in the canteen on her own, Vicky took in the looks from the people around her and sighed. What had seemed like a heroic role in helping the people of Home suddenly had a very different taint to it.

# Chapter Nineteen

Flynn had come back to the room he shared with Vicky late the previous evening. He must have been in the canteen because Vicky had gone for a second workout and hadn't seen him outside the gym. When he entered the room, Vicky lay awake in the dark and watched his silhouette slip into bed. The creak of the flimsy metal frame issued a catcall of moaning springs. He obviously didn't want to talk, so Vicky pretended to be asleep.

When she woke up the next day, he'd already gone. If she'd have searched the canteen, she probably would have found him. Instead, she skipped breakfast, kept her eyes straight ahead when she walked through the dining area, and headed for the front door to meet Hugh.

At the other side of the canteen, Vicky climbed the stairs to the small foyer and Home's exit. Early, she stood in the space alone and stared out the window at the long grass. At about waist height, the sun lit up its tips, highlighting the vibrancy of the green field. The warm image stood in contrast to the touch of the cold glass when she rested her forehead against it.

Hypnotised by the field as it danced with the elements, Vicky let the window steam up from her warm breath.

A voice called out behind her and Vicky spun around to see Hugh walk up the stairs with a girl of no more than about fourteen behind him. "Right," he said to her. "I need you to let us out and then wait here until we get back so you can let us in again, you got that?"

Quite sharp in the delivery of his instructions, it clearly intimidated the slim and pale girl, who said nothing but dipped a curt nod at him.

"Good. Now don't mess this up because we'll die if you do. Our lives depend on you, okay?"

The girl nodded again and her already pale skin turned translucent. She looked like she could vomit at any moment.

Before Hugh could say anything else, Vicky walked over to the girl and lifted both of her hands. She waited for the girl to look up, the wide blue orbs of her scared eyes finally taking Vicky in. "Don't worry, darling, I know you can do this. We won't be too long, so all you have to do is keep an eye out for us and open the door when we get back. You'll be fine, okay?"

The girl nodded and Vicky beamed a smile at her. "Atta girl."

"Okay," Hugh shouted. His booming voice made the girl jump from the ground. Any of the tension Vicky had helped her release returned with interest. "Open the door, sweetheart."

Although Vicky shot Hugh a glare, he seemed oblivious to it or, at the very least, chose to completely disregard it.

The girl visibly shook as she fumbled with the bolt at the top of the door and Hugh tutted at her.

"Fucking hell, Hugh," Vicky said. "She's a kid, give her a fucking break, yeah? I know you're frustrated at the moment, but don't take it out on her."

Tears glazed the girl's eyes as she looked at Hugh and it seemed to take the edge off his aggression. A slight nod at the girl and he said, "Please open the door."

When he looked back at Vicky, Vicky nodded at him.

The *crack* of the first bolt called through the open space, followed soon after by the *crack* of the second one. The large metal hinges moaned their protest as the girl pulled the door open, and the fresh outside air whooshed into the small foyer. Vicky stood in the glorious breeze and drank in the fresh grassy rush of it. It had only been a few days since she'd breathed outside air, but it felt like a lifetime. A lot of the stress and stagnation within her body washed away, and Vicky stood taller than she had done in a while.

Hugh led the way and stepped outside. Just before she followed him out, Vicky reached over and touched the top of the girl's arm. "Don't fret, love, you'll do just fine when we need you to. See you soon, yeah?"

The girl nodded and Vicky turned her back on her to head outside.

The breeze in the doorway had been heavenly, but the unfiltered wind outside of Home bordered on orgasmic. For the briefest second, Vicky allowed herself the luxury of closing her eyes and felt the wind against the exposed parts of her skin. It rushed over her face and billowed in her ears. She clenched and unclenched her hands and it danced through her fingers. When she opened her eyes, she found Hugh staring at her. "What?"

"Are you okay?"

"I spent ten years outside. To live in a windowless hole is quite restricting by comparison."

A slight smile lifted on Hugh's face. He then thrust his large arms out to the sides and pulled a deep breath in through his nose, which raised his wide chest. "It sure does feel good, doesn't it?" he said on the exhale. After a glance around, he added, "But come on, we need to get going."

Hugh doubled back to walk up the hill that led over the top of Home. Vicky followed him. When she'd caught up to him, she said, "I know you're getting frustrated with how much you have to do, and I can see how the responsibility of Home is incredibly stressful. Also, I know I've only been here a few days—"

"Spit it out, Vicky. I have thick skin."

Not that she'd seen evidence of his thick skin, but Vicky said it anyway. "Do you think you could stop being such a dick? It's not good for morale."

Hugh's jaw dropped and he looked at Vicky. Something close to rage burned in his eyes until he swallowed it down. After he'd looked around them again, he laughed to himself and shook his head. "That's why I'm pleased you're my deputy."

"Huh?"

"I need someone to say that to me. Not many people would. Thank you."

A shrug and Vicky looked out for the diseased as she waited for Hugh to continue.

Hugh's breaths became heavier as he walked up the hill and he panted between his words. "You're right, I have been a dick. I need to relax a bit and manage my stress in a more productive way. I just feel so *responsible* for everyone's lives, and they don't seem to give a shit about anyone but themselves."

"But like with any relationship, you have to accept the part you play in it," Vicky said.

"What, I *should* look after them?"

"No. You *do* look after them."

"So their laziness is my fault?"

"You give them a comfortable existence and you've not asked for anything in return. That's an amazing thing. But when you need something back from them, you need to remember that you've not required anything from them for a long time. To you or me, what they need to do is obvious and you'd hope they'd offer it freely. But for them, they need a period of adjustment before they can become the people you need them to be."

While Vicky spoke, Hugh scanned the area again. The long grass could be hiding the diseased; although, despite the wind, they should hear them coming. Besides, at about three feet tall, the grass would only hide children and the smallest of adults. Both of which would be easy to outrun should they get surprise attacked.

At the top of the mound, Vicky looked out over the sea of black. "Was it three hundred and twenty-two solar panels?"

"Three hundred and twenty-seven," Hugh corrected. "Enough to power this place forever as long as we look after them."

The grass around the panels had been trampled. "We'll need to stamp the grass down again," Hugh said. "I don't want it messing with the panels in any way."

As much as she tried to resist, Vicky looked over at the spot where she and Jessica had dumped the bitten woman. A gust of wind threw the reek of rot at her. More pungent than the tang of the diseased, Vicky ruffled her nose against it. Although several corpses lay in the same place, Vicky looked at the woman, her mouth spread wide in what seemed to be a silent scream, her eyes dried pits in her face. "What will we do with the two men that came into the community the other day? How long can we keep them locked up for?"

A shrug and Hugh shook his head. "I really don't know. We have to let them out at some point. I'll talk to Jessica and see when she feels comfortable with it. She spends most of her time with Serj, so they won't be able to sneak up on her and attack her. I hope they'll have had time to reflect and can see that Jessica did the right thing." A nod at the corpse below them and Hugh said, "That woman needed to be taken out."

The zip on Hugh's jacket creaked when he tugged it, pulling Vicky's attention from the pile of bodies and back to the man. He then passed her a once white, now brown, towel.

The thing hung limp in Vicky's grip. "What's this?"

"It's what we have to do today."

Vicky said nothing in reply and Hugh elaborated. "We need to clean the solar panels. These things are our life source. Without them, we're fucked. I clean them every few weeks. Now I have help, we can get it done in half the time."

The spaces between the solar panels created a maze of walkways. Vicky thought about the swarm of diseased that had rushed through them to get to her. She drew a deep breath as she scanned the horizon.

"Let's get this done, then," she said, and ran down the grassy bank to the first of the panels.

# Chapter Twenty

Despite the threat of the diseased hovering over them, the day passed without incident. They had spent anywhere from two to four hours outside, but now Vicky stood next to Hugh in the monitor room of Home, she finally relaxed. "It felt good to get out there today. I know it's dangerous, but I've missed being outside."

"Maybe if we get some of the people outside, they'll remember that feeling too," Hugh said. "UV lights and recycled air can keep them alive, but they could have so much more."

As Hugh spoke, Vicky watched the monitors. The black and white grainy images showed a still world beyond the front door of Home, a haunted world. "When do you think the diseased will die out?"

"I thought they would have been gone within the first six months. Shows what I know, huh?"

Vicky didn't reply. She'd thought the same thing. Had she known then that a decade later she'd still be the minority species on the planet, then maybe she wouldn't have had the fight to see it through. It didn't bear thinking about how long the diseased would last for. They knew how to hunt and they seemed more resilient than humans, so maybe they would end up being the dominant species on Earth.

When Hugh spoke, it snapped her from her daze. "You wanna record the next radio broadcast?"

Vicky remembered sitting in her container, listening to her windup radio, and her mouth dried. "What will *I* say? Who knows how many people are listening to that message, pinning their hopes on a better life. I'm not sure I could do it justice."

"You could maybe tell your story briefly. Show other people that they're welcome here. Be an inspiration to them."

When Hugh handed a Dictaphone to Vicky, she took it and smiled. It made sense that she should do the next broadcast. She cleared her throat and pressed the record button. "If you're anything like me, you've found a radio of some sort and you're living in some kind of hole or tree house or barricaded in the basement of an old mansion." After a slight pause, she relaxed a little. "Wherever you are, I bet you don't have enough food, you have no electricity, and you haven't had a warm shower in years. When I heard my first broadcast from Home, I knew I needed to come here, and I'm glad I did. I've been here for less than a week and it's the most comfort I've had since the outbreak. They have beds, warm showers, electricity, running water, and food. All we ask of those who come here is that you're prepared to help out and that you come with peace in your hearts. We're a thriving community and we want to continue to grow our numbers. The diseased aren't going anywhere. To beat them, we need to take the fight to them. Come and join us in taking our world back."

After she'd pressed the stop button, Vicky handed the Dictaphone back to Hugh, who smiled from ear to ear.

"That's nice to see," Vicky said.

"What?"

"You smiling. It's been a few days. It's nice to see it return."

"It's nice for it to return." Hugh then said, "I saw the way you looked at Jessica when she brought the dead animals to the kitchen. We have some weapons locked in a room in one of the back corridors. Wanna go out hunting tomorrow?"

Vicky smiled and nodded several times. "Yes! I sure do."

# Chapter Twenty-One

They reached one of the many locked doors and Vicky stood back as Hugh opened it to reveal the room beyond. When she saw the rack of baseball bats along the back wall, she grinned. "Oh my!"

With a nod, Hugh swung his arm into the room as if to invite Vicky to enter. She took him up on his offer and walked in.

As she'd seen from the corridor, one wall had been exclusively dedicated to bats of all shapes and sizes. Baseball bats, cricket bats, rounders bats. Despite her urge to reach out and grab one, Vicky turned to take in the rest of the room. A small section of crossbows, some longbows, knives, swords … Vicky paused as she looked at them. When she reached out for the shotgun, Hugh said, "Don't bother."

Stopping mid-reach, Vicky turned to the man. "Huh?"

"We ran out of cartridges a long time ago. They're useless now. We keep them in case we find more ammo, but I don't think we will. Besides, the noise attracts the attention of the diseased anyway."

"So when I first came here and you had one …?"

"Yep, it was empty. The sight of them, like the gas masks, tends to give us the edge we need when bringing new people into Home."

After she'd shaken her head at Hugh, Vicky looked at all of the weapons again. When she saw a catapult similar to the one she'd used herself, she reached out and grabbed it. She slipped it into her back pocket, the familiar press of it against her butt offering her a reassuring calm. She also picked up a baseball bat and a crossbow.

"You can shoot one of them things, can you?" Hugh asked as he looked at the bow, his eyebrows arced in a slightly condescending manner.

"What are you saying? That because I'm a woman I can't shoot? Of *course* I can shoot one of these, can you?"

A wry smile and Hugh laughed as he shook his head. "Chill your boots, love. I've seen you fight; I don't think you being a woman impairs you in any way shape or form. I was merely saying it because I can't shoot them for shit. I think they're a nightmare."

Vicky laughed and then winked at him. "Maybe I can teach you one day."

The apparent stress of the past day or so seemed to have lifted from Hugh's burdened shoulders, and he grinned back at her, a sparkle in his eyes. "Maybe."

Now Vicky had loaded herself up, she watched Hugh lift a katana, an axe, and a catapult also. When he lifted a brown sack about the same size as a bag of sugar, it jangled like it contained glass. He passed it to Vicky, who opened it up and grinned broader than before when she peered inside. "Oh my." The glass orbs—some milky white, some silver, some swirled with greens, reds, and blues—stared back up at her. "Marbles! Where did you get these from?"

"There were plenty of toy shops left with all of their stock in. Marbles have to be the perfect ammunition for a catapult, right?"

But Vicky didn't reply. Instead, she stared at the bag of marbles for a few seconds longer before she tied it to her belt.

A chill gripped a hold of Vicky and snapped a shiver through her. The room clearly remained locked most of the time, so it wouldn't ever have the chance to warm up. When she looked up to see Hugh watching her, she smiled at him and he smiled back.

"You ready to go?" he said.

Just before Vicky nodded for them to leave, she saw what looked like a harness of sorts. It hung on the same peg that she'd retrieved her crossbow from. "Is that …?"

Hugh nodded.

After she'd handed her crossbow to Hugh, Vicky grabbed the harness and slipped it on. She then took the heavy crossbow back and fitted it so it clung to her back. A couple of pulls adjusted the straps so it sat tight against her body. "This'll make things a lot easier!"

With her catapult in her back pocket and her bat in a two-handed grip, Vicky turned to Hugh. "Okay, I'm ready now."

\*\*\*

A group of four young people between the ages of about ten and fourteen sat in one corner of the canteen. Unlike adults, who would often mirror one another with their body language, they all sat in different poses as if fighting for their identity among their peers. When they looked up at Hugh and Vicky approaching them, they fell into line, all of them straightening their backs and their eyes widening at the sight of the two heavily armed guards. The girl from yesterday sat among the group and she blushed when she saw Hugh.

A glance at Hugh, and Vicky saw his stern expression. She elbowed him, which threw him a little off balance. "Smile at them, for God's sake. They're kids and you scare the life out of them."

Although Hugh tried to do as Vicky had asked, it looked more like a pained grimace than a warm gesture. He managed the kind of greedy smile cannibals would flash their victims. For the briefest moment she thought of Zander at the shopping mall and her skin crawled. A shake of her head banished the image and Vicky strode out in front of Hugh so the kids could see her rather than him.

"Hi, guys," she said when she got close enough.

None of the kids replied, their eyes shifting from Vicky to Hugh and back to Vicky again.

"We need some help on the front door again today. Hugh and I are going out hunting, and we need to make sure we have someone there to let us back in when we return."

The group remained silent.

A glance around the canteen and Vicky saw that she and Hugh were the focus of everyone's attention. And why wouldn't they be with the amount of weapons they had on them?

Vicky turned back to the kids, all of them frozen in their seats. "Come on, then, let's go."

The kids did as they'd been ordered to and they all got up. Without a word, they followed Vicky and Hugh up the stairs to the entranceway of Home.

At the top of the stairs, Vicky and Hugh waited for the reluctant gang to join them. The girl from the other day visibly shook in Hugh's presence.

"We've brought four of you up here," Vicky said, "so you can take it in shifts. Two at a time, we need you looking out for us until we return. Maybe do your shifts in three-hour slots, okay?"

"How long do you think you'll be?" one of the boys asked before he instantly flushed red.

He jumped when Hugh responded instead of Vicky. "Hopefully not too long. But you never know with these things."

What were rosy cheeks drained of their colour and the boy dropped his attention to his feet.

"Right," Vicky said, "any more questions?"

The kids shook their heads as one.

"Good."

After she'd snapped the two bolts free, Vicky pulled the door wide and let the breeze toss her hair. Just inhaling the fresh air made her heart kick in her chest as her life essence surged. She let Hugh out first and said, "Just make sure you see us when we come back, okay?"

Again the kids responded in unison, nodding their agreement at her.

After Vicky had stepped outside, she stared out in front of Home while listening to the door close behind her and the locks slip back into place. Stood in the fresh breeze, she drew another deep lungful of the clean air. A kick of adrenaline surged through her, sharpening her senses and heightening her awareness to both prey and predator.

# Chapter Twenty-Two

The pair had walked for about fifteen minutes through the long grass before the river that Vicky had crossed on her way to Home came into view.

"I dread to think how many more diseased we'd see were this river not here," Hugh said.

Whilst staring at the body of water—her trousers damp with dew—Vicky thought about her solitary journey to Home after she'd left Flynn.

The strong wind stung Vicky's eyes and she blinked several times to ease her discomfort. She then looked at her surroundings. In such an overgrown world, the diseased could come from anywhere. Despite the beauty of the lush and vibrant landscape, she couldn't forget that every long patch of grass or overgrown bush could conceal a diseased waiting to attack.

When Vicky got closer to the river, she looked down. Two large blue barrels that had been bound with wood and vines had been dragged up the riverbank. "That must have been the raft Flynn used when he came here."

"Huh?" Hugh asked.

"He can't swim."

The confused frown lifted from Hugh's face. "I suppose they don't have Sunday morning swimming lessons at the local leisure centre anymore."

"Exactly."

Tracks ran away from the makeshift raft down into the water, and Vicky imagined Flynn on his own, dragging the vessel out as the diseased called at him from the other side. The burn of tears itched her eyes and a lump swelled in her throat. "I can't believe I left him. The poor kid must have been petrified."

Hugh said nothing as the sound of moving water washed between them.

After a deep breath, Vicky said, "We may as well use the raft, eh?"

Hugh grinned at her.

"What?"

When he looked at a tree close to them, Vicky snapped, "*What*? What are you looking at?"

Still without a word, Hugh walked over to the tree and stuck his hands into the leaves that coated its trunk. When he pulled a thick rope out, weighted with a lump of wood that had been tied horizontally along the bottom of it, Vicky smiled too. "That would have saved me a lot of hassle had I known it was there. Flynn too."

"It would have been on the wrong side for you."

"That's true."

Hugh sheathed his sword, put his axe beneath his right arm, slipped the swing between his legs, jumped backwards to add to his momentum, and flew out across the river. Mid-swing, Hugh shifted, so when he arrived at the bank on the other side, he slipped off and landed on the grass, the rope still in his grip.

Vicky moved over to where Hugh had swung from and waited for him to throw the swing back to her.

Minus the weight of a fully grown adult, the swing only just made its return journey. On the edge of her balance, Vicky hooked the rope, her stomach lurching from the prospect of a fall into the water below.

For a few seconds, Vicky held the swing and stood with her feet firmly on the ground. Then, as Hugh had done, she sat on the swing and launched herself across to the other side.

Were Vicky not so concerned with staying dry, she might have enjoyed the exhilaration of the ride. Instead, she tried to copy Hugh in adjusting her position halfway over the river, and when she came to the bank on the other side, she slid from the seat and leapt for it, the swing still in her right hand, her baseball bat in her left.

Although she landed on the bank, she'd hit the ground as the swing headed back the other way. The momentum pulled her toward the river, and for a moment, everything dropped into slow motion.

Several clumsy steps and Vicky held onto the rope as it dragged her back toward the water. She couldn't let it go. Not after Hugh's ten point zero landing. Although, as she hopped on one leg ever closer to a wet plummet, she loosened her grip. Rather the rope than her.

Just before she completely let it go, she came to an abrupt stop. Anchored by her belt, Vicky turned around to see Hugh grinning at her again as he held her in place with a tight grip on the back of her trousers.

Vicky stared at Hugh and Hugh stared back. Neither spoke. Maybe she'd been wrong not to trust him.

Because they'd been staring at one another for too long to be comfortable, Vicky shook her head, handed the swing to Hugh, and walked past him. She looked out in the direction they were headed. They couldn't switch off to the danger of the diseased. Not even for a second.

# Chapter Twenty-Three

As they walked, Hugh shook his head and laughed again. "Your face on that swing."

"All right, Dick Grayson."

A confused frown came Vicky's way and she batted the comment off with a wave of her hand. Comics meant little to society ten years ago, let alone now. "Don't worry."

For the past ten minutes, Vicky had been able to see the huge buildings on the horizon, and for the past ten minutes, she expected them to take a diversion. "At the risk of sounding soft—"

Hugh looked at her.

"—we're not going in *there*, are we?"

The long grass swished from both the wind and the path the pair cut through it. The humour left Hugh's features and he said, "Of course we are. Where else do you think we should go?"

The old city stood on the horizon as a ghost of what it must have once been. Many buildings had been reduced to skeletons from fire. Those that hadn't been burned stood ragged with neglect. It didn't look much different from Biggin Hill by the time they'd left it, but Vicky knew Biggin Hill; she'd spent a decade there and she'd watched it deteriorate.

"Do we need to go in there to hunt animals? Wouldn't it be better out in the open?" God, she sounded like Flynn the first time he left the airport.

"Firstly," Hugh said as he pulled up to a stop next to her and held his hand at about chest height, level with the tops of the grass, "look at how tall this grass is. Anything could hide in here and we wouldn't have a hope in hell of seeing it, let alone killing it. Secondly, the cities seem to attract the animals to them. Almost like they expect to find something worth scavenging like they did a decade ago when humans did nothing but produce waste."

Both points seemed valid, and when Vicky thought back to Biggin Hill, her best hunting had come from within the town. Besides, she knew this world. She knew the diseased. Sure, she didn't know the city in front of her, but she knew how to deal with the threats that no doubt waited inside it. Hell, even with Hugh's army training, she could probably deal with it better than he could.

When Vicky didn't reply, Hugh nodded and set off again through the long grass.

\*\*\*

As with most main roads that entered big towns and cities, this one sat as a wide mess of cracked asphalt. Nature had destroyed the upper crust of the road as grass grew through it. Slowly determined—like the tortoise—nature had won where humans had tried to oppress it. The buildings—covered in vines and leaves, walls cracked from where plants grew through them—showed how nature had wrapped a strong grip around the throat of human architecture. What had seemed like permanent structures were being consumed by the environment.

The road ahead forked left and right around a huge office building. At least ten stories tall, the round front of the building faced them.

Vicky's jaw fell loose as she looked up at the top floor. "The view must be amazing up there. I can't imagine that space would have been cheap to rent when property had value."

What used to be windows now stood as empty spaces. Each one had been smashed and there remained no trace of the glass that once filled them. The strong wind tore through the steel structure and a cacophony of tones wailed at them, a ghostly choir singing a dirge for the town.

So large and prominent, many of the buildings Vicky had seen from outside of the city now sat hidden behind the vast structure. "It must have been a sight before the world went to shit."

Not quite as enamoured by the massive building, Hugh nodded as he looked around them. "It looked like many towns back then. Full of soulless offices made from steel and glass. It shone like a diamond but contained junk. Insurance brokers, traders, gas and electricity companies … they all added to the bullshit of the society we left behind. I used to watch the suited workers walk in and out of that place like they were serving time."

"I know how that felt," Vicky said.

Before she could say another word, Hugh snapped a hand

across and grabbed her forearm. It took all Vicky had not to call out in fright. When she looked at Hugh, he pointed at the large building.

Although Vicky looked at the structure, she couldn't make out what he'd seen. Clearly aware of her confusion, Hugh spoke from the side of his mouth. "First floor. There's a fox."

Squinting to see into the shadows of the first floor, Vicky spied the mangy canid and pulled her catapult from her back pocket. Once she'd loaded it with a marble, she went to take aim, but stopped when Hugh nudged her. "This is mine."

"Will you hit it?"

A deep scowl and Hugh returned his focus to the ginger beast.

After she'd lowered her catapult, Vicky watched the man next to her and kept the marble pinched in the weapon.

With one eye closed, Hugh raised his catapult and looked down it into the building. His chest rose with a steadying breath before he loosed the catapult with a *thwack*. The marble whooshed away from them in the direction of the fox, but before it got to it, it caught one of the building's metal window frames with a loud *ting*.

In the near silent city, the sound carried like an early morning church bell.

Before the ring had stopped, Vicky had lifted her catapult, pulled it back, and loosed her shot. The fox raised its head at the sound of Hugh's marble just in time for Vicky's to catch it square in its left eye. A wet pop and the creature fell on its side.

\*\*\*

Swollen with the smug feeling of showing Hugh up, Vicky took off toward the building at a sprint. The marble had hit the fox true, but experience had taught Vicky about birds in the bush. She wanted this fucker in her hand.

The crossbow on her back swayed from side to side as she ran up to the office. It clipped the metal window frame when she jumped through the space, and the crunch of the broken remains of the window popped beneath her steps on the inside. She heard Hugh crush more of the broken glass when he followed her through.

The open-plan office sat laid out probably as it had before everything went to shit—old computers sat on desks with cheap chairs close to each one; yellowing bits of paper littered the office floor. Some desks had discoloured photos that had probably once shown the owner of said station a beaming picture of their loved ones. They would have provided photographic motivation as the workers endured the mind-numbing servitude to a capitalist master, a way to remember why they were there in the first place. As Vicky weaved through the desks, she glanced to either side. She couldn't see any diseased, but experience had taught her not to take it for granted. The fuckers could come from anywhere at any time.

The double doors at the end of the office had the handles on Vicky's side. There had been too many times where she'd tried to get through a building quickly and had shoulder barged a door that didn't go the way she expected it to. She now looked for handles before she made that painfully bad decision.

When she got to the doors, she pulled one of them open and ran into the stairwell on the other side. Before the door fell closed, Hugh had followed her through.

The carpet that had once covered the stairs now sat torn and rotten in many places. Vicky watched her feet to make sure a flap didn't trip her up.

On the first floor, she shoulder barged the door and burst through.

The ginger fox lay on its side close to the large window through which Vicky had shot it. As Vicky closed down on it, she saw its chest swell and deflate with its rapid, panicked breaths. Even unconscious it seemed to feel the fear for its life. Before it could feel anymore, Vicky came upon it and slammed her boot down on the creature's head. Its skull cracked and crumpled as the fox fell limp beneath her heavy stamp.

Relieved at killing the beast, Vicky sighed and relaxed for what felt like the first time since she'd entered the town.

One of the straps on the harness wrapped around Vicky's waist like a belt. She unbuckled it so both sides of it hung down. A quick shake showed her the harness seemed secure enough without it. Vicky then proceeded to tie the fox to one of the limp straps before she let the small beast hang from her. It might have been an extra weight, but it was the best way to carry it at that moment.

When she opened her mouth to address Hugh, who'd finally caught up with her, the shrill screams of several diseased stopped her dead.

Vicky walked over to the smashed window on the first floor and looked down at the road they'd used to enter the town. Her blood ran cold.

Twenty to thirty diseased gathered below; with their mouths

open wide, they stared up through dried bloody eyes.

The glass crunched beneath Hugh's feet as he came and stood next to Vicky. After a long exhale, he said, "Oh fuck."

# Chapter Twenty-Four

When Vicky got halfway toward the doors that led to the stairwell, she checked behind her and froze. Hugh hadn't moved. Instead, he stared out of the window, his arms limp by his side.

The frenzied screams of the diseased got closer as they rushed at the building like a tsunami. A range of frequencies, they called and yelled, their feet beating thunder against the road outside.

"Hugh," Vicky called, "hurry the fuck up, will ya?"

Nothing.

"Hugh!" This time so loud it tore at her throat.

Still nothing.

"Fuck it." Vicky ran back at Hugh, weaving through the discarded office furniture to get to him.

When she caught up with him, she whacked him so hard with her open palm that he stumbled forward. "What the fuck are you doing, you fucking idiot? We need to run. Now!"

The sound of the diseased rushing into the building below seemed to break his fear-induced paralysis. Their cries echoed through the ground floor.

When Vicky took off again, Hugh followed this time. The pair ran back toward the double doors that led out into the stairwell.

The diseased had a head start on them, and as Vicky ran, the power left her legs. It seemed hopeless, and it had been made a million times worse by the fact that Hugh couldn't get his shit together.

When Vicky reached the double doors, she grabbed the handle and yanked them wide. As she stepped out into the stairwell, she heard the mob crash into the doors below; a rattling smash ran up the stairwell as they tried to push them open.

Without breaking stride, Vicky ran up the stairs to the higher floors.

"What are you doing?" Hugh called up after her.

With her attention on where she headed, Vicky shouted over her shoulder, "I'm running away from them. You have a better idea, do you?"

Silence met her question. She then heard the heavy breaths and clumsy steps as Hugh ran up the stairs after her.

The doors on the ground floor banged several more times as Vicky and Hugh climbed higher. The diseased, clumsy and uncoordinated, struggled to finally get the doors open. Their screams of frustration shrieked through the enclosed space when they eventually managed it.

By the time they'd reached the top floor, Vicky's legs burned with fatigue and her lungs felt fit to burst. Stars swam in her vision from the effort, and sweat stung her eyes.

She waited outside the doors to the top floor until Hugh

caught up with her and she watched him rush straight through them, but she didn't follow. Instead, she pulled her crossbow from her harness and loaded up the first of her ten bolts.

The doors to the office reopened and Hugh poked his head out. "What are you doing?"

With one eye closed, Vicky bit down on her bottom lip and took aim. "I'm giving us a chance." She squeezed the trigger and the crossbow kicked as it shot the bolt.

The projectile flew down the space in the middle of the stairwell and hit one of the diseased in the shoulder. It screamed, but didn't slow down.

With shaking hands and out of breath, Vicky loaded another bolt and called to Hugh, "Go and find us a way out while I slow them down."

Vicky kept her attention on the seemingly never-ending pack as they ran up the stairs. She pressed the crossbow stock into her shoulder again and let another bolt free with a loud *crack*! This one went straight through the eye of one of the lead diseased and knocked it backwards, sending a couple of its peers back down the stairs with it.

It only stalled their ascent; by the time Vicky had the third bolt loaded, the pack had resumed their climb. Another kick and another snap of the crossbow's bolt and Vicky hit another diseased in the arm.

Four, five, six bolts, and the seventh scored another killing blow. Not quite the lead diseased, but one close to the front. It stalled the rush of the mob but nothing more than that.

Vicky stood on her own at the top of the stairs with three bolts left. Each bolt scored a more damaging blow to the snake of fury that rushed up at her, slowing the pack some more.

Just a couple of floors separated Vicky from the diseased. The concrete stairs seemed to vibrate with the stampede of the monsters. So close, their fetid reek of rot and decay swirled around her. A slight heave caught in Vicky's throat, and she took off through the double doors that led to the top floor.

On the other side—the sound of the mob slightly diminished through the closed doors—Vicky put the nose of her crossbow on the ground. Several kicks later, she broke the bow away from the body and discarded it before wedging the body through the door handles to block the diseased from coming through. It didn't look like it would hold them for long, but it would give them a little more time. She then ran over to Hugh at the other end of the top floor.

Like on the first floor, Hugh stood at the edge of the building and looked out over the town below them.

The curve at the front gave a panoramic view of the road and fields they'd crossed to get to the town. Because every window had been smashed and they stood so high up, the wind crashed into Vicky, blowing her hair back. "What are you doing, Hugh?"

The glazed look of fear had returned to the ex-army man's eyes. Door-kicking in Mogadishu had sounded like utter tripe at the time, but now that she'd seen how he reacted in a tight situation, Vicky knew he'd been bullshitting her for sure.

However, when she looked out over the town below, she couldn't see an escape route either.

Before she could say anything, Hugh finally spoke. "We have nowhere to go. We're fucked."

As if to drive the point home, the doors that led to the stairwell crashed and shifted inwards, pushing against the broken crossbow from the weight of diseased on the other side. They needed a plan and fast.

# Chapter Twenty-Five

Several white bars ran like a row of bumpers around the edge of the building on the top floor. Each one slightly further out than the one before it, they spread out to form a ledge, the spaces between each one smaller than the length of Vicky's foot. They stuck out from the building by about an extra metre. The whack of the double doors met the crossbow's resistance again, and Vicky looked everywhere else for a way to escape, but she kept returning to the bars.

The slight rip of splintering wood tore through the room and Vicky spun around to look at the doors. They'd been pushed so far forward, a wide gap ran down the centre of them. Several arms reached through the space and dirty fingers clutched at the air. Screams, moans, and a rotten stench reached through with them. They only had one choice, and the sooner Vicky made it, the more time they'd have to execute it.

With the fierce wind blowing her hair out behind her, Vicky stepped toward the ring of white metal bars. Flecked with rust, each had a diameter of about ten centimetres, and they looked strong enough to hold the weight of an adult.

With Hugh frozen and gormless by her side, Vicky knew she'd have to do something where the Mogadishu door-kicker couldn't.

Fuelled by the sounds behind her, Vicky edged forward. The strong wind shoved her back a step, but she dipped her head and pushed on again.

What used to be floor-to-ceiling windows now stood as a huge open space that made it easy for Vicky to walk out onto the white bars.

The first step outside threw Vicky off balance again. The wind had been funnelled straight into her by the building, but now it came at her from all angles.

At the end of the bars, Vicky sat down, her stomach lifting to the roof of her mouth as she looked at the ten-storey fall. She took several deep breaths and dangled her legs over the edge. A glance over her shoulder at Hugh and she saw he remained exactly where she'd left him.

"What the fuck are you doing?" he called at her.

"I'm getting out of here. I suggest you follow me unless you want to die."

"I ain't going out there!"

Another *boom* came from where the pack of diseased hit the double doors, and after he'd spun around to look at them, Hugh suddenly changed his mind and moved toward Vicky.

Vicky twisted around and grabbed the bars to her left with two hands. Her heart hammered its way to cardiac arrest.

Ignoring the shake in her arms, Vicky slipped from the ledge and let her body fall. Gravity tugged on her frame and she swung down. About halfway through the swing, her arms snapped tight and she twisted in the air so she faced the ninth floor below. The metre protrusion of the bars hadn't seemed like much when Vicky had been on the tenth floor, but as she looked at her landing site on the ninth, it seemed like a mile.

With a strong grip on the bars, Vicky hung down, the wind swaying her. A few seconds later and Hugh seemed to have found his military courage, because he joined her, hanging at her side. The pair shared a glance before Vicky watched Hugh look into the ninth floor. He clearly understood the plan.

At that moment, the crossbow creaked and split, and the sound of the diseased flooded into the tenth floor. When Vicky lifted herself in a pull-up, she saw the rush of the monsters as they came at her.

In a matter of seconds, three of the front-runners sprinted out onto the bars and continued forward. One of them stood on Vicky's hand as they all plummeted over the edge and fell to the ground below with a *thump,* quiet because of the distance of the drop. The others seemed more cautious. Despite the sting in her hand, Vicky held on.

Using her legs as a pendulum, Vicky rocked back and forth as she gripped onto the bars. The wind messed with her motion, and although her body went mostly toward the window space below, she certainly didn't swing true.

With most of her focus on the ninth floor, Vicky noticed Hugh as he swung next to her, copying her every move.

The agitated cries of the diseased called at them from the tenth floor, but they persisted as they swung back and forth, gathering more momentum each time.

At full swing, her legs out behind her, Vicky looked down to see the three broken forms of the fallen diseased below. It served as a stark reminder of what an error in judgement would cost her.

On her third swing forward, the wind in her ears, the diseased furious that they couldn't get to her, Vicky let go, weightless as she leapt.

# Chapter Twenty-Six

Every one of Vicky's internal organs seemed to tense as she flew through the air toward the ninth floor.

When she crashed down, her legs gave way beneath her and she fell forward. Her knees smashed against the floor so hard it felt like she'd shattered both of her kneecaps.

Despite her pain, Vicky got to her feet and turned to Hugh, who continued to swing from the bars. "I can't wait here forever, Hugh. If we don't leave now, we lose our advantage."

With his eyes pressed so tightly closed they threw crow's feet around the sides of his face, Hugh muttered to himself.

Vicky bounced on the spot and listened to the diseased above. The sight of Hugh seemed to hold them in place, but for how long?

Once he'd opened his eyes again, Vicky saw a clarity in them that she hadn't seen since the diseased picked up their tail.

On the next swing forward, Hugh let go and fell toward her.

As Vicky stepped aside, Hugh crashed down on the hard floor.

Without any time to waste, Vicky grabbed his arm and

pulled him to his feet before she shouted, "Come on, let's get out of here."

Although clumsy in his pursuit, Hugh followed Vicky's lead as she sprinted through the office to the stairwell doors at the end.

After she'd ripped the doors open, Vicky let Hugh run out first. The man flew past her and straight down the stairs to the lower floors.

Vicky gave chase, the sound of the infuriated diseased still above them.

Although their feet beat a tattoo down the partly carpeted steps, the sound paled in comparison to the slam of the ninth floor's double doors. The loud *crack* echoed through the stairwell and the raucous diseased fell silent in response to it. Why hadn't Vicky taken the time to close it quietly?

A second later the diseased's footsteps rushed across the tenth floor. In a blink, they'd appeared at the top of the stairwell and stared down at Vicky and Hugh a few floors below them.

When Vicky saw Hugh stop to look up, she fought for breath and called down to him, "Run, you fool. Get to the ground floor, now."

With no need for stealth, Vicky watched Hugh leap the last four or five stairs of each flight to speed up his descent. She did the same, each landing slapping the dead fox against her thigh and running a hard jolt through her already sore knees.

It seemed to give them the edge, and once they'd gone down several floors, they seemed to have opened up a lead on the diseased.

Vicky's lungs felt ready to burst, her face burned with sweat, and her head spun, but she pushed on after Hugh.

On the ground floor, Hugh shoulder barged his way through the double doors and held one of them open for Vicky to follow him. Vicky tore through with the sound of the diseased coming after them. She saw the fear in Hugh's wide eyes. If this guy had had military training, he'd forgotten it all. Either that, or he'd never seen a battle in his life.

Before she tore out of the ground-floor office, Vicky stopped and Hugh pulled up in front of her. "What's wrong?" he asked.

Without a word, Vicky moved over to Hugh and took the axe that he had strapped to him. Like she'd done on the top floor, she used the weapon to wedge through the handles of the double doors. "That should hold them for a while," she said as she ran back past Hugh and out of the office.

At the end of the ground floor, Vicky hurdled through the empty window space, the crunch of glass popping beneath her feet.

Hugh followed her out onto the cracked asphalt of the broken main road and they ran from the town at a sprint. It took for Vicky to step out into the strong wind to realise just how stagnant with rot the air in the office had been.

Now they'd gotten a slight lead on the diseased, Vicky noticed the dead fox more as it slapped against her thigh. She laughed. "All that for a bloody fox."

Hugh didn't reply.

# Chapter Twenty-Seven

Back outside the large town, Vicky and Hugh had slowed down to a walk as they waded through the high grass. With her arms out to the sides and her palms raised to the sun, Vicky drew the deep breaths that she associated with freedom. To fill her lungs with fresh air reminded her that she'd avoided another near miss and remained disease-free.

The grass around them swayed and bowed and her hair danced in the wind. As much as she loved the security of Home, it came with challenges such as recycled air and no windows.

Worry lines creased Hugh's face from clearly still feeling the stress of their encounter in the derelict office block. Ten minutes had passed and Vicky's pulse had only just settled down too. He looked across at Vicky and dropped his head with a sigh. "Have you heard of PTSD?"

"Post-traumatic stress disorder, of course I have."

"I suffer with it. Sometimes I wake up in the night in a cold sweat as I remember what I went through during my service."

He hadn't seemed like a military man. In the way he moved and in how he spoke, almost with a glorification of what he'd done. The few military people Vicky had known in her life played down their tours, but Hugh seemed to revel in them. But what did Vicky know? She'd not met enough military people to gauge it. Besides, he had nothing to gain from lying. "So what exactly did you do in Mogadishu? Door-kicking makes it sound like you were some kind of unorthodox bailiff."

The same haunted look that had glazed Hugh's eyes when he'd frozen in the office block returned to his distant stare. A slight tremble ran through his voice. "I can't talk about it. It's classified."

"Classified in a world that no longer exists?"

As he snapped his head across to look at her, Hugh raised his voice. "I took an oath. I don't expect you to understand what it means to take it, but I *do* expect you to respect me when I say I can't talk about it. At some point, the military may come back. When they do, I want to be able to return to them with a clear conscience."

The less Vicky asked, the easier she found it to believe Hugh. It made life a lot simpler if she didn't doubt him. With that in mind, she shrugged at the man. "I don't know much about PTSD. All I know is that when I'm in a tight situation like we were today, I need to know the person with me has my back."

Although Hugh looked like he wanted to shout, he ground his jaw and said nothing.

With the tension wound tight between them, Vicky heard something in the distance. The wind battered her and made it hard to hear. However, when Vicky looked back toward the ruined town, she didn't need to rely on her hearing. "Fuck!"

Hugh looked behind too at the swarm of diseased that ran

through the field. At least twenty strong, they had Vicky and Hugh in their sights.

"Come on," Vicky said as she broke into a run. "Let's get the fuck out of here."

\*\*\*

The repeated slapping of the fox against Vicky's thigh had started to bruise her. The run made it sting more than ever, but she didn't have a better place for it at that moment.

At the wide river, Vicky fished the rope swing from where they'd left it. She held it out for Hugh, who batted the offer away as he gasped for breath. "You go first and I'll follow."

They didn't have time to argue, so Vicky did as Hugh instructed and swung across the river.

Hardly graceful, when Vicky landed on the bank on the other side, the earth soggy as it gripped onto her feet, she fell forward onto her knees. The wet mud soaked through her trousers and felt cold against her skin. It coated her hands, the thick sludge of it between her fingers. As she got to her feet and wiped herself down, Vicky suddenly saw what she'd done and her heart sank.

On the other side of the river, Hugh stared fury at her as the rope swing hung limp between them.

The call of the diseased grew louder behind Hugh, who turned around to look over his shoulder.

As she looked from the swing to Hugh and back to the swing again, Vicky shook her head. She couldn't get it back to him. She had no fucking chance. Then she saw the diseased break through the long grass just a few metres from Hugh.

After one final look over his shoulder, Hugh leapt out into the muddy water of the river.

Several diseased followed him in, throwing themselves from the high riverbank on top of him as he swam across. Where Hugh had been visible in the water, he suddenly went under, dragged down by the swarm of drowning diseased.

The loud splashing around Hugh and the agitated roars from the diseased on the other side of the river swirled in the panic in Vicky's mind. Her heart thudded in her throat and her head spun. She'd killed him.

A loud gasp burst through her panic and Hugh broke the surface of the dark water. He fought to remain afloat as he flapped and splashed. He looked at Vicky.

Before Vicky could react, Hugh disappeared beneath the surface again. It looked like he'd been dragged back under.

Vicky remained perfectly still and frowned so hard it darkened her view of the world in front of her. The water—churned up and muddy from the struggle—rushed with the flow of the river, but Hugh didn't reappear.

A full minute passed and Vicky's throbbing pulse rocked her where she stood. The water turned an even darker shade of brown while Hugh remained beneath the surface. At what point would she walk away like she'd done with Flynn?

# Chapter Twenty-Eight

The muddy water cleared and the diseased on the riverbank stared across at Vicky, snarling and hissing, but more muted in their aggression toward her than they had been. They seemed to accept they couldn't get to her. Agitation shimmered through their ranks as they rocked from side to side and bit at the air like they could taste her, but even that they did with less enthusiasm than a few minutes ago.

As Vicky watched the spot of water where Hugh had vanished, her eyes stung from not having blinked. With her heart in her throat, she waited. Although what she waited for … Surely Hugh would have come up by now.

The sound of the diseased died down and the noise of the wind picked up as if to highlight Vicky's solitude. Before long, she'd have to make the choice to return to Home alone.

The sting in her eyes turned into an itch of tears and her bottom lip bent out of shape with her grief. Hugh might have had his failings—an ego that drove him to work out like he did and to lie to Vicky about his service—but he didn't seem like a bad guy. Just a bit naïve in his outlook on life. But …

Before Vicky could finish her thought, a loud splash broke the surface of the water and she stumbled backwards. The mud grabbed her feet and she fell. Although the wet ground provided a softer landing, it still jolted from Vicky's coccyx all the way up her spine. Not that she had time to worry about her pain. Instead, she scrambled backwards, her feet slipping in the mud as she fought to get away from the diseased that had made it across to the other side.

With her attention on the river, she saw the monster's head break through the surface of the water. Then she stopped. "Hugh?"

Coughing and spluttering, Hugh emerged from the river, heaving for breaths as he climbed up the bank toward Vicky. At first he said nothing, the effort of his escape clearly too much for him, but once he'd stepped completely free from the water, he smiled. "I hope you hadn't given up on me?"

With a shake of her head, Vicky jumped to her feet, ran over to the man and wrapped him in a tight hug. He stank of river water and squelched in her tight embrace. But Vicky had lived in this world long enough to keep a hold of her wits. She released him and stepped back a pace. "Have you been bitten?"

"Huh?"

With a pointed finger thrust at the water, she said, "I saw several diseased drag you beneath the surface. It's a reasonable question. Have you been bitten?"

Hugh laughed and shook his head. "No, I haven't."

But Vicky needed more than that. "Show me."

At first, Hugh didn't respond; he simply stared at her. "Don't be ridiculous, Vicky. Why would I lie?"

"For the same reason that everyone lies. No one wants to believe they'll turn." She loaded her catapult with a marble, pulled it back, and aimed it straight at Hugh's face. "I don't want to do this, but I need to make sure you've not been bitten. I'm not risking the safety of Home by taking someone back who could change into one of *them*. I'm not suggesting you need two days' quarantine, just that *I* need to see you're okay."

A wry smile played with Hugh's lips as he lifted his top to reveal his washboard stomach. "Okay, I'll play along."

Once he'd taken his top off, he stood on the riverbank with his wide shoulders and pecs on display and continued to grin at Vicky. With her jaw clenched tight, she kept the catapult aimed at him.

"Oh, like that, is it?" Hugh undid his belt and fought against the wet fabric of his trousers as he forced them down to his ankles. He then turned on the spot. Like his upper body, his legs had the definition of someone who worked out a lot. He sure had the shape of someone who'd been in the military, even if he didn't have the story or mentality to back it up.

"Do I have to take my shoes off, or do you trust they couldn't bite through these boots?"

Before Vicky could respond, Hugh grabbed the waistband of his boxer shorts. "Hang on, you need the money shot, don't you?"

Vicky finally lowered her catapult and raised a halting hand at him. If he had a bite, she would have seen it by now or at least the blood from the open wound. "It's fine, just show me your ankles and then we're done."

"That's a shame," Hugh said as he pulled his trousers up

again and did the belt up. After he'd lifted his trouser legs and rolled his socks down, he said, "Happy?"

A nod and Vicky turned her back on him. "Fine, let's go."

"You know what?" Hugh called after her as she walked off. "I'm impressed at your vigilance. You really do value Home. We'll make a guard of you yet. And maybe when we get back, you can inspect me for bites again."

Without turning around, Vicky threw Hugh the bird and kept walking.

# Chapter Twenty-Nine

The pair had walked in silence for five to ten minutes before Hugh said, "Are you sure you don't want to check me again for bites when we get back to Home? Just to make sure."

"That sounds like a good idea," Vicky watched Hugh visibly prick up at her response. "Although, I think I may get Piotr to perform a thorough inspection while wearing a pair of his gardening gloves."

When Hugh screwed his nose up, Vicky couldn't help but laugh at him. With the dead fox still strapped to her, the creature slapping against her leg with every step she took, Vicky looked at the darkening sky. "Good job we got out of that town when we did. I hate travelling anywhere at night."

The grass swished as Hugh walked through it and looked up at the sky. "I've never had to. Although, it's not something I'm keen on doing either."

"How far from Home have you been?"

"A few hours' travel, no more."

"Have you been to the mall?"

"No, but I've heard of it."

"Flynn and I spent a night there."

Hugh stopped and looked at Vicky. "And you came away with all your limbs?"

Vicky stopped too. "So you know what they do there?"

"Of course."

"And you do nothing about it?"

Tension gripped Hugh's face. "What would you have me do? We have a community full of freeloaders that slip a disc every time they tie their shoelaces. Home's strength is also its greatest weakness. Such a solid fort, it's made everyone weak and unable to fight."

"But …" The words left Vicky. But what? What could they do about it?

Vicky made a quick search for diseased before she nodded toward Home. "Come on," she said. "Let's get back."

Within a couple of steps, Hugh had caught up with Vicky. "I didn't say I don't care about what goes on in the mall. I do—I absolutely do. It's not natural—but they have their town that they raid and we have ours. If I upset them, we stand to lose much more than they do. They'll tear straight through us."

"Okay, you've made your point. Atrocious things have happened and continue to happen. I don't like it, and I'm sure you don't either, but I'm not sure I agree about not taking action. At any moment, that band of cannibals could decide to turn on Home and you'd be easy pickings for them. I always think you should strike first."

"Right," Hugh said, slightly out of breath from trying to keep up with Vicky's fast march. "Maybe you can help us form a plan that sees us taking the fight to them."

"I would, but you don't need to worry about them anymore. It's the principle I'm pissed off about."

"You've taken them down?"

"The disease got them," Vicky said. She then focused in front of her as they rounded the next bend and Home came into view.

"How did you manage it?"

Vicky said nothing. She didn't need to relive what she and Flynn had gone through in the mall.

"I think you have a point though, Vicky. Any enemy that threatens our way of being needs to be met head-on. Phase three, right? Phase one, get them fit; phase two, get them used to being outside of Home; phase three, protect ourselves."

Only about ten metres from the front door of Home and two loud cracks snapped through the relative quiet. Vicky then heard the hinges on the large reinforced door groan.

Despite the bruise on her thigh, Vicky had kept the fox strapped to her and she picked her pace up to a jog to get back through the open door.

Only now, as she viewed herself through the wide eyes of the two teenagers who'd let them back into Home, did Vicky realise just how different she looked compared to when she'd left earlier that day. Dirty, sweaty, minus a crossbow, and with a dead fox strapped to her. And Hugh, still soaked from his swim, his boots covered in mud, and his features slack with fatigue. If the way she felt was anything to go by, Vicky no doubt looked just as burned out.

When they entered the foyer, the air already staler than that outside, the teenagers locked the door behind them and slipped the bolts back across. Without looking at them, Vicky undid the fox she had strapped to her and passed it to Hugh. She then removed the crossbow harness with the baseball bat still wedged through it then pulled out her catapult and bag of marbles. She handed the lot to Hugh and rolled her shoulders, glad to be free of the extra weight.

Swamped with all of her kit, Hugh raised an eyebrow at Vicky.

"I assume you can drop these off on your way back to your room?"

Before Hugh could answer, Vicky smiled, said, "Thanks," and walked off.

# Chapter Thirty

The second Vicky entered the room, Flynn said, "So more people are using the gym now." He clasped his hands together in front of his chest. "I feel so fulfilled."

At first, Vicky didn't respond to his facetiousness. Tired from her day, but grateful for the freshly washed grey tracksuit that had been left for her, Vicky lay back, sank into the groaning springs of her bed, and looked straight up at the ceiling. "That's nice."

"I've been stamping pieces of paper *all* day."

If the boy wanted a fight, he should just fucking start one. "Good, so we've found a good use for you, then?"

Silence.

Something about Flynn's teenage petulance pushed Vicky's buttons and she couldn't help but goad him. "Hugh will be pleased with all the good work you've been doing. He might even get you a more comfortable chair or maybe a stamp with a bigger smile on it."

"Yeah, it's great work. Really putting me to good use at that desk. In fact, I think I've found my calling."

"Wonderful. I'm so happy for you."

"Fuck off, Vicky."

Despite her tiredness, Vicky sat bolt upright in bed and stared at Flynn. "*What* did you just say to me?"

Red-faced and with pursed lips, Flynn continued to stare at her, but he didn't reply.

From his expression, Vicky could see that he knew he'd overstepped the mark, but she couldn't let it go. "Would you have spoken to your parents in that way?"

Flynn's eyes narrowed. "No, but you're not one of my parents, even though you like to think you are."

In a more Zen moment, Vicky might have taken the outburst with the pinch of salt it deserved. An emotional kid, Flynn said the words because he'd wanted to hurt her. But it had been a long and tiring day. "Would you have preferred I left you back at the containers on your own?"

"Maybe I might have done better."

"You'd have died within a week, Flynn. Get your head out of your arse, boy, and grow the fuck up, yeah? You have this job outside the gym because we don't want you to die. I love you more than any other person I've loved, and whatever you think of me, I think of you like a son. I will die protecting you. If protecting you means you hate me for a while, then so be it. As long as you're alive."

Vicky's response seemed to disarm Flynn, who shrugged. "You said you wouldn't leave me again."

"And I won't."

"Then *why* did you go out today?"

"What I mean is that I won't give up on you again like I did.

Ever. If there's a chance for you, I'll die trying to save you. If I could go back to that bunker we were in, I'd fight every one of the diseased to get to you. But you have to accept that I need to leave Home from time to time."

Although Flynn didn't respond, his tense form had relaxed somewhat.

Vicky had wanted to tell him about her day, but she didn't want him to realise how dangerous her trips were. Or to give him any reason to doubt Hugh. Until she had some stronger evidence about the man, she wouldn't say a word. She lay back down again, and as she relived the day to herself, her limbs grew heavier with tiredness and her breaths more shallow.

Every blink lasted longer than the one before it as sleep took her over. She spoke with slurred words. "How about I talk to Hugh about getting you a more interesting job?"

"Forget it," Flynn said.

As much as Vicky wanted to respond to him, her eyes had started to sting from exhaustion. With her brain grinding to a halt, the slightest flash of compassion went with it. She had to say more to Flynn, but she couldn't fight it and slipped into sleep's warm embrace.

# Chapter Thirty-One

When Vicky woke, her entire body ached. The previous day had been hard on her and not worth the one fox they returned with. But she'd gotten to know Hugh a little better. She now knew what the man did and didn't have, and she trusted him less. Too many things didn't add up. Despite his impressive physique and clear physical fitness, she couldn't rely on him when shit went down. Maybe Flynn needed the chance he so desperately craved. Regardless of his skill level—which had become much higher than Vicky would be prepared to admit to him—he would follow her into hell if she needed him to. Hugh wouldn't.

"I've been thinking," Vicky said as she looked across at the bed next to her … but it lay empty. Flynn must have got up already. Although cloudy in her memory, the previous evening came back to Vicky. She'd fallen asleep while talking to him about how unhappy he was. "Shit," she muttered. "Way to show him you care."

Vicky sat up a little too quickly and her head spun. For the next few seconds, she sat on her bed and stared into space.

Standing up with more caution, she slipped her khaki guard

uniform on, the fabric scratchy compared to the smooth grey tracksuit she'd changed out of. One last look at Flynn's empty bed and she left the room. The first stop would be to find Flynn and make sure she hadn't upset him too much. Then she could find Hugh and work out what they had planned for the day.

\*\*\*

The sound of conversation and cutlery hitting crockery swam in the high ceiling of the canteen. If she didn't have any responsibility, Vicky would have rested up for a day, her eyes on fire from lack of rest and her movements sluggish. But she'd signed up to help run Home and she had to take everything that came with that. The good and the bad.

Although she couldn't see Flynn, Vicky sat down to knock back a bowl of cereal. The breakfast shift would close soon and she didn't want to have to wait until lunch before she ate something.

The bland cereal and watery milk crunched with every bite. Magnified through her skull, it added yet another sound to the busy cacophony in the canteen.

It took no more than a few minutes for Vicky to eat her cereal. The second she'd finished, she took the bowl to the huge pile of dirty plates and cutlery, dumped it, and left the room.

\*\*\*

"It's always the last place you look, eh?" Vicky said as she walked down the corridor toward the gym and found Flynn sat outside at his desk.

"What is?" the boy replied, a slight edge of impatience to his tone.

"The thing you're looking for."

"I'm a *thing* now, am I?"

"You know what I mean."

"And of course it's the last place you look," Flynn said. "You'd hardly carry on looking for something after you'd found it, would you?"

A moment's pause and Vicky smiled at him. "How are you today?"

"Fine."

The sound of the treadmills and the exercise bike came from the gym. When Vicky peered in, she saw three twisted faces and smelled three sweating bodies. None of them seemed to be deriving any pleasure from their visit, but at least they were making the effort. Before she could say anything, a man stepped off the bike. In his late forties to early fifties, he had closely cropped hair—although most of it had already fallen out—and a large paunch.

Wheezing as he left the gym, the fat man handed his book to Flynn to stamp—both of them apathetic about the transaction—before the man stumbled away, a towel wrapped around his shoulders and a smile stamped on his record card.

The reek of body odour left with the man, and as Vicky screwed her nose up in response to it, Flynn said, "Hugh's opened the showers permanently now. He said they should be able to sustain them, and he'd keep an eye on the water situation in case he needed to ration them again. But he couldn't stand the stench."

"Have you seen him this morning?"

Flynn opened his mouth to respond, but before he could

make a sound, a call came from back down the corridor. "Vicky."

She looked back to see Hugh approach them, a frown on his chiselled face.

"You have to come with me. I have something to show you."

"What is it?" Vicky asked.

"Just come with me, yeah?"

She looked back at Flynn, who scowled at her. He'd opened up to her for a short time, and now that she had to suddenly go off, he looked hurt all over again.

\*\*\*

Hugh led Vicky to the cells where they'd kept the two men who'd arrived with the bitten woman.

Vicky shrugged. "So. What is it?"

Hugh shoved one of the doors open with his foot. The hinges creaked as it rolled inwards, and when Vicky looked inside, she gasped, "It's empty."

"As is the other one."

"Where have they gone?"

"Jessica."

"Huh?"

"Jessica let them out. She said it had been two days and they deserved to be treated like all of the other people in Home."

"But …"

"I *know*," Hugh said.

"So, what, we trust them like Jessica has?"

"I don't know what we should do. I mean, Jessica's the one most at risk, and she's okay with it."

"And we can't exactly lock them up again."

"Right?"

A heavy sigh and Vicky shook her head. "I don't like it."

"Nope, me either."

But what could they do? Jessica had made the choice.

"So where are they now?" Vicky said.

"Fuck knows," Hugh replied.

"Jessica just set them free to go wherever they wanted?"

A nod and Hugh sighed. "Not the way I would have done it."

"I reckon we should go to find them at least and see what's going on with them. I think these two will need steering toward becoming good citizens. I'm not ready to trust them yet."

"I agree," Hugh said.

# Chapter Thirty-Two

After a search of Home, Vicky and Hugh returned to the gym. They stopped by Flynn's table and Hugh asked, "Have you seen two men you don't recognise?"

"I don't recognise most people. What do they look like?" Flynn asked and then threw Vicky a glare.

"One of them's tall, blond, and has bloodshot eyes," Hugh replied. "The other one's short and has brown hair."

"He looks a bit like a troll," Vicky added.

Another look at Vicky and Flynn turned to Hugh. "Have you tried looking in the canteen?"

"We've looked in the canteen, the kitchen, the medic bay, and all of the empty rooms. Hell, we even checked the foyer in case they decided to leave and left the front door open."

"Who are they?" Flynn asked.

"A couple of men we had in quarantine. Jessica decided to let them out." A glance into the gym and Hugh leaned closed to Flynn so he could speak in hushed tones. "I think they could be dangerous to the community. But keep that one under your hat, yeah? The last thing we need is an unnecessary panic."

Vicky kept her smile to herself. Hugh didn't need to do that for Flynn, but by including him in their search, he'd given him the respect he so craved. And he'd done it without prompting from Vicky.

A serious expression and Flynn nodded at Hugh. "Okay. I'll let you know should I see anything."

After he'd patted Flynn's shoulder, Hugh walked down toward the farm at the back of Home and Vicky followed after him.

When they'd gotten out of earshot, Vicky said, "Thank you."

But before he could reply, Hugh stopped dead.

When Vicky looked up the long corridor, she saw it too. Close to the farm at the end, two men stood in plain view.

Hugh picked his pace up and Vicky marched with him. When they got close enough to smell the damp earth on the other side of the farm doors, Hugh cleared his throat and the two men jumped as one and looked around.

"Are you okay, gents?" Hugh asked.

The tall one—the blond scruffy mess—still had bloodshot eyes like he'd had too much to drink. The short stocky one still looked like he'd be better living beneath a bridge than in Home.

Neither man spoke as they stared at Hugh.

When Vicky stepped forward, she caught the dirty smell of the two men and snapped her head back. She did her best to hide her revulsion as she said, "Is there something you're looking for?"

Silence met her question.

"Look," Vicky said, "what the fuck are you doing back here?"

The blond man coughed. "We're hungry and the canteen's closed. We haven't eaten properly for a long time."

"We fed you while you were in the cells," Hugh said.

The men looked at one another. "We're both still starving."

With her hands on her hips, Vicky glared at the men. "So you thought you'd go snooping around the place?"

"Look," the shorter of the two said. "We didn't mean any harm, honest. We just wanted to see if we could find some more food. We've not been here long and thought it was rude to ask for seconds in the canteen."

A faster pulse and rage rising in her chest, Vicky stepped forward another pace, despite their reek of ground-in dirt. "So you thought you'd steal some instead? That's less rude, is it?"

"As long as we don't get caught, yes."

Before Vicky could say anything else to the men, Hugh cut in. "Look, this is a community with rules and laws. We have cells because we have to have them, but we don't like to use them if we can avoid it. How about we start again, yeah?"

Neither man replied.

"Also, I have a job for you two. Not today, but when you've had time to recover, I want to use you to clean the solar panels each day. Unlike most of the people here, you've been outside recently, so I want to make the most of that."

The tall blond man stepped forward. "You want us out there *again*?"

"We all have to do our bit to keep Home running."

"And who's to say you won't lock us out when we leave?"

"If we'd wanted you gone," Hugh said, "we wouldn't have let you in in the first place. There's a bed for everyone at Home;

that includes you as long as you do your bit and don't cause trouble. Besides, if you're prepared to go outside, then you're more useful than most of the people here. Why would we kick that out?"

Dark stares fixed Vicky and Hugh, dark stares from sunken eyes that had already known too many hardships.

The stand-off held for a few seconds too long, and Vicky reached for a weapon she didn't have.

Finally, the shorter man of the two nodded at Hugh and Vicky. "You won't get any trouble from us."

Hugh let the silence hang before he replied, "You two should go back to your rooms and get some rest. Everyone gets a couple of days to acclimatise. Enjoy it. Oh," he added, "and have a shower."

The men shuffled past Vicky and Hugh like scolded teenagers. Dragging their heady smell, they watched their feet as they walked.

Once they'd disappeared from sight, Vicky leaned close enough to Hugh to smell the soap on his skin and spoke in a whisper. "I think we've got our work cut out with those two."

# Chapter Thirty-Three

The snap of the door handle cracked through the room, forcing Vicky awake with a panicked inhalation as if she'd been drowning. In one scrabbled movement, she sat bolt upright in her bed, whacked the light on with the palm of her hand, and pushed her back into the wall. She had nothing to defend herself with, so she pulled her knees to her chest and stared at the doorway.

Although a shocking vision stood before her, she recognised the man. The starkness of his panicked glare damn near sprang from his face as he gasped for breath, unable to get his words out.

Instead, he raised his shaking hands to show them covered in blood.

"What the hell?" Vicky said and looked across to see Flynn in the bed next to her, his body language mirroring hers.

"I …" Hugh tried, but another rush of panicked breaths stole his words.

The dry taste of morning locked in Vicky's mouth, and she swallowed several times to clear it a little before she said, "It's okay, Hugh. Sit down and tell me what's happened."

But Hugh backed away from her and shook his head. "You need to come and see for yourself."

The stress of the situation had taken Vicky's self-consciousness away, and only now, as she sat with Hugh in front of her, urging her to get out of bed, did she realise she had just a vest and knickers on.

Her guard uniform lay on the floor by her bed, so Vicky reached down for it. She pulled her trousers on beneath the covers and then her shirt. She nodded at Hugh. "Fine, take me to where we need to go."

Flynn jumped from his bed too, and he and Vicky locked stares. The order for him to stay put sat on the end of her tongue, but Vicky saw pain shimmer across Flynn's eyes in a pre-emptive reaction to her rejection, and she swallowed it down. "Hurry up and get changed, then, if you're coming with us."

A stoic nod and Flynn dragged his tracksuit on.

\*\*\*

Bleach hung heavy in the corridor as it always did, and other than the footsteps of the three of them, Vicky heard nothing else. Whatever the time, most people were still asleep.

Hugh stopped outside one of the many rooms along the corridor between the kitchen and the farm. Not a holding cell, storage room, or the gym, it must have been empty like most were in the back half of Home.

With the blood on Hugh's hands, Vicky had a strong idea of what she'd find, just not who. Still without a weapon, she nudged the door open with her foot, the slightest squeak of the hinges echoing from the action.

But the door didn't open fully. Instead, it swung into the room and stopped, as something lay in the way of it. A dry gulp and Vicky swallowed again immediately afterwards as if the second attempt to rehydrate her throat would offer something more effective. A shake had taken a hold of her limbs as she pushed the door as wide as she could open it and peered around to see what blocked the way.

A frigid wash of gooseflesh covered her skin when she looked down at the body and the large glistening pool of blood it lay in. With panic galloping through her chest at the strong metal stench of spilled blood, Vicky fought to get her words out as she said, "Jessica? My God, Jessica."

Had she seen him come in, then maybe she would have done something about it. But she didn't, so before Vicky knew it, Flynn had entered the room next to her and he too stared down at the expired form of Jessica.

Pale to the point of translucency, Hugh came into the room and finally managed to force some words out. "I found her like this." With his bloody hands raised, he shook worse than before. "I did everything I could to help, but she's gone, Vicky; she's gone."

Before Vicky could respond to him, Jessica gasped on the floor and the three of them jumped back.

"Quick," Vicky shouted. "We need to get her to the medic bay now. Help me."

Vicky dropped down into a crouch next to Jessica and stroked her hair away from her face as she stared into the woman's glazed glare. "It's okay, honey, just relax and we'll get you to the medic bay."

Very little recognition ran through Jessica's distant eyes, but she nodded like she understood. With blood everywhere, Vicky scanned the woman for the location of her wound. The most blood seemed to come from her middle, but Vicky couldn't be sure where exactly. When she slipped her hands beneath Jessica's body, one along her lower back and one just beneath her bum, she called up to the other two, "Hugh, Flynn, one of you get the legs, and one of you get the head and shoulders.

With the other two in place, Vicky nodded at them. "Okay, on three. One, two, three …"

They all lifted Jessica from the ground, and blood dripped from her like water from a full sponge.

Both Hugh and Flynn stared at the mess that rained down onto the floor.

"Right," Vicky said. "We need to get to the medic bay *now*."

At the front, holding Jessica's head, Flynn led the way out into the corridor.

\*\*\*

After they'd placed Jessica on the medic bay's bed, Vicky opened and closed each one of the drawers in the small unit beside it. Once she'd finished, she turned on Hugh and threw her arms up in the air. "Not even bandages? Seriously?"

A shrug and Hugh looked at Jessica, worry creasing his brow.

Although Jessica breathed, her respiration came in shallow waves that diminished by the second.

"You two," Vicky said to Flynn and Hugh. "Take your tops

off. We'll use clothes as bandages." She then ripped Jessica's shirt open to reveal her flat stomach. A quick count and she saw at least seven deep red stab wounds. Each one belched thick blood like tar coming from a bog. The metallic stink of it mixed with what smelled like human waste.

When Flynn held his grey tracksuit top in Vicky's direction, Vicky took it, looked back down at Jessica, and physically sagged. She watched Jessica's head loll to the side, and her breathing dropped to the faintest whisper. "Who am I kidding? There's no way she's surviving this."

Jessica then opened her eyes, stared at Hugh, and mouthed soundless words at him. Her mouth worked frantically and she shook her head, but the effort of communicating seemed to take it out of her and she fell back down against the bed a second later.

Despite the thick blood that coated her hands, Vicky ran two fingers along Jessica's neck and felt the last kick of her pulse. Jessica released a final breath and fell limp. Vicky dragged a white sheet over the woman. Within seconds, the fabric had turned red with her blood.

Grief locked in Vicky's throat as she stared at yet another dead friend. One of many to pass, Vicky's sadness added to the swollen lump in her oesophagus that had existed since everything went to shit in this world. The burden of yet another death.

When Vicky turned around, she saw a crowd had gathered in the kitchen and they all watched on. Although they stood still, statuesque in their observation of the dead Jessica, Vicky caught movement behind them.

"Coming through," a male voice called. "Please let me through. Guard coming through."

Before she saw him, Vicky's heart sank. A second later, Serj broke the line of the crowd and locked eyes with Vicky. Tears burned Vicky's eyes as she watched the realisation sink through Serj's features. When he looked back up at her, she bit onto her quivering bottom lip and shook her head.

"No," he said and stepped forward. "Please, no, not Jess. Jess?"

Vicky pulled a stuttered breath in and tried to speak to Serj, but the lump in her throat wouldn't let her. Instead, she stood aside as the man strode over, a slight hobble still in his walk.

When he pulled the white sheet back, he stared down at Jessica's corpse for what felt like the longest time before he released a roar of a wail. The loud and broken cry sounded like he'd had his soul torn from him.

With tears streaming down his face, he screamed, "No! No! No!"

As the one who knew him best, Hugh should have stepped forward to offer the man comfort, but he didn't. Instead, Flynn walked over to Serj and put an arm around his shoulders. In moments like that, words had no place. The sixteen-year-old boy got that and didn't even try. The sight of Flynn comforting Serj set Vicky off worse than before and her grief cascaded from her.

# Chapter Thirty-Four

They stood over Jessica's dead body and Vicky watched Serj's face turn red as he shook his head. "She shouldn't have let those mongrel fucks out of their cells. I knew this would fucking happen."

Before Serj could walk away, Hugh grabbed his arm and the two men glared at one another. For the briefest moment, Vicky readied herself to step between them, but the aggression died down when Hugh spoke in a soft tone. "Let Vicky and me go to see them. We have to remember that we're part of a community, and we can't assume people are guilty until we've put them through a trial."

The distressed Hugh of moments earlier had suddenly vanished, and Vicky couldn't help but notice how his grief had all but left him.

"Are you fucking serious?" Serj said.

Hugh looked at the crowd of at least fifty people gathered in the large room.

It seemed to prompt Serj to do the same. He sighed before he lowered his head and spoke to the floor. "Okay."

"Now," Hugh said. "Why don't you and Flynn go to look for evidence in the room where she was killed? That is, if you want to get involved in this investigation? Otherwise you can leave it to us."

When Serj lifted his head again, he fixed a stare on Hugh and fire burned in his eyes. "Of *course* I want to get involved."

Although Vicky remained on edge as she watched the two men, Hugh thankfully didn't respond to the confrontation.

With Jessica's blood continuing to soak through the white sheet, Vicky stepped away from Hugh and Serj, grabbed another sheet from the side, and covered her over with a second layer. Bad enough that they had a dead body in Home, they hardly needed the sight of all that blood too.

Fortunately the bed had wheels, so Hugh grabbed it to take her away.

Just as he went to push it off, Serj blocked his path. "Where are you taking her?"

"I need to lock her in one of the spare rooms. We can't leave a dead body lying around."

Despite grinding his jaw as he stared at him, Serj didn't argue with Hugh. After a few seconds, he stepped aside to let him through.

The men seemed to be getting nowhere fast, and their animosity toward one another spoke of a conflict Vicky knew nothing about. It made sense for Serj to be upset, but why did he blame Hugh? Maybe he had the same gut feeling as Vicky. But her instinct made no sense. Why would Hugh kill Jessica? The grief of the situation had to be messing with her head.

"Flynn will show you were it is," Vicky said, Jessica's blood pulling the skin on her hands taut as it dried.

With the sensitivity of a man rather than a boy of sixteen, Flynn gently tugged on Serj's arm. "Come on, let's start the investigation so we make sure we find the people responsible for this."

After they'd walked off, Vicky spoke in a whisper so only Hugh could hear her. "Do you think the two prisoners did it?"

Hugh raised his eyebrows while he pushed the bed. He then whispered, "What do you think?"

A rhetorical question, Vicky looked over at the crowd of people. It seemed obvious who had killed Jessica, but maybe a little *too* obvious. Whatever they concluded from their investigation, they owed it to the community to conduct one. The people of Home had to see that punishment only came after rational enquiry, not before.

The wheels on the bed squeaked as Hugh pushed it across the vast open space of the kitchen. All of the onlookers had gathered by the corridor farthest away from them, so Hugh headed for the one closest. The less the community saw of the dead body, the better.

Maybe Vicky had imagined it, or maybe the shock of what had happened caused the sensation, but as she walked behind Jessica, the smell of blood hung so rich in the air, she was sure she could taste it on the back of her throat like it were her own.

# Chapter Thirty-Five

After they'd found an empty room and locked Jessica's body in it, Vicky and Hugh headed for the rooms of their two main suspects for Jessica's murder. They walked in silence for a few minutes before Vicky broke the tension. "What was that about with you and Serj?"

Hugh looked across. "Huh?"

"There seemed to be a lot of beef between you two."

A shrug of his shoulders and Hugh kept his quick pace, his boots clicking on the hard floor as they marched down the corridor. "I think Jessica used to like me, and Serj finds that hard to deal with. I suppose in the old world, you just moved away from the people that made you feel inferior. Now you have to live and work with them."

The arrogance threw Vicky off, but when she looked at the tall and toned man next to her, she could see how he'd make other men feel inferior. Were Serj the kind of person Hugh had just described him to be, then the beef between them made sense. But Serj didn't seem to be that kind of person.

Inside Home, Hugh never seem fazed. So when they got to

the door of one of the men and he drew a deep breath that seemed designed to calm his nerves, Vicky's heart fluttered. What would be waiting for them on the other side of the two doors?

Vicky moved down to the room next door so they could take a man each. As one, her and Hugh knocked, the sound carrying in the sleepy corridor. Despite the crowd in the canteen, a lot of the residents would still be dozing.

It took a few seconds, and just as Hugh lifted his hand to knock again, the door in front of him opened. A couple of seconds later and Vicky's door opened too.

The shorter of the two men appeared in front of Vicky. A lumberjack of a man, he stood bleary-eyed and scratched his head. "What's going on?"

With the press of a machete slipped into the back of her belt, Vicky stared at the man. Hugh held one similar, which he also concealed behind him. They'd agreed they'd only show them if they had to. It seemed better that they didn't start out by waving huge blades at them. "Can you please step out of your room?"

"Huh?"

"I don't want to have to ask you again," Vicky said.

The man—dressed in just his boxer shorts—stepped out into the corridor. The tall, blond man in front of Hugh did the same.

The room on the opposite side of the corridor could be locked like so many in Home. After he'd kicked it open, Hugh said, "You need to get in there, please."

The taller man frowned. "You want to lock us up again? No fucking way!"

When Hugh pulled his machete free, the man raised his

hands in defence and walked into the room. His short mate followed him in at the sight of Vicky's blade.

As Hugh locked the door on them, one of the two called from the other side, "What have we done? Why are you locking us up again?"

But Hugh ignored them. Instead, he pointed at the room he intended to enter and said, "I'll search this room; you search the other one, yeah?"

Not sure what to look for, Vicky nodded anyway. "Okay."

Although similar to the room Vicky shared with Flynn, the room of the shorter man seemed dirtier in just one night than hers and Flynn's had been in several. Clothes had been thrown on the floor and it stank of stale farts. Standing as far away from the duvet as possible, Vicky leaned across and grabbed it in a pinch. The smell seemed worse for disturbing the man's bed, and Vicky tensed in anticipation of the noxious reek she was about to release. She counted silently down from three and snapped the duvet away. Fortunately, the smell didn't get any worse.

Before she could search anywhere else, Hugh's cry stopped her dead. "Come here, Vick."

He'd never called her that before. It shouldn't have bothered Vicky, but something about the sharp truncation of her name grated. A shake of her head and she went next door to find Hugh, a grim set on his features as he held up both a bloody kitchen knife and a silver chain.

"This is Jessica's necklace. And I found this knife. I suppose the good thing about living in a closed community is that it makes it hard to hide shit like this."

It seemed short-sighted of the blond man to have the knife and chain in his room. Surely if he'd done it, he would have found somewhere better to hide the evidence.

Hugh had brought a clear plastic ziplock bag with him, which he slipped the two items into before he walked over to the locked room on the opposite side of the corridor. "Right, I want you to come out one at a time. I don't care who comes first, work it out between yourselves. We both have machetes and aren't afraid to use them."

Vicky heard shuffling on the other side of the door. Hopefully it signalled the two men deciding who would go first and nothing else.

With her machete in her hand, a white-knuckled grip on the wooden handle as if it would stop the shake than ran through her, Vicky watched the door. Her throat felt dry.

Just before Hugh unlocked the room, he passed a bag of white cable ties to Vicky. She pulled one out and waited.

The click of the freeing lock ran both ways along the corridor, and Vicky's furious heart lifted into her throat. If the blond man had killed Jessica, he might not come out easily. He had nothing to lose now.

After Hugh had opened the door, the blond man stepped out, his eyes as bloodshot as always, his hair a bird's nest of chaos. He didn't look like someone who had just been rumbled.

The other man remained in the room, allowing Hugh the time to close the door and lock it again. He then pointed at a wall for the tall man to walk over to and took a cable tie from Vicky. As Hugh bound the man's hands, he pressed against the man's back and said, "I'm arresting you on suspicion of murder.

You will be tried in our court." He then held the clear bag up in front of the man's face. "Although I don't think a trial will do you much good. Why didn't you try to get rid of the weapon you stabbed her with?"

The blond man raised his voice. "What the fuck are you talking about? I've never seen that knife before."

Before he could say anything else, Hugh shoved him hard into the wall he had him pressed against. The blond man connected nose first, a wet crack resulting from the impact. When he pulled away, a line of blood ran from his nose, over his lips, and dripped off his chin.

"Save your bullshit for when you're on trial." As if to show the man he had no power, Hugh tugged his wrists back so they lifted away from his body. The man leaned forward and drew a sharp breath across clenched teeth. In no position to retaliate, he stared at the floor and said nothing.

After they'd got the second man out of the locked room and Hugh had bound his wrists with the makeshift cuffs, they led them back to the prison rooms they'd stayed in when they first arrived at Home.

Some of the crowd who'd gathered in the kitchen remained there. All of them watched Vicky and Hugh lead the two men through.

As if taking his chance to appeal to as many people as possible, the shorter of the two men said, "Look, I don't know what he did or didn't do. I can't say because I was in a different room. But if he did do anything, it had nothing whatsoever to do with me."

A hurt look pulled on the blond man's features when he

stared at his friend. "I didn't *do* anything."

"I'm not saying you did. I'm saying that I had nothing to do with whatever's happened and that I haven't been with you."

"Whatever," Hugh said. "You two come as a pair. You'll both be tried for Jessica's murder."

The shorter of the two men said, "But—"

"Shut the fuck up," Hugh said. "Save it for your trial, yeah? The community will decide whether you're guilty or not." A glance at the gathered crowd and Hugh said, "And you're not making yourself look very good in front of them at the moment."

As much as Vicky wanted to stick up for the two scruffy men, she couldn't. They seemed innocent, but how could she level a charge against Hugh when she had nothing to back it up with. Before she challenged the man, she had to have sufficient evidence to make her case watertight. After all, she was about to go up against the leader of this community.

## Chapter Thirty-Six

Vicky fought for breath as she climbed the steep hill with Hugh beside her. She didn't know where she was, and Hugh didn't seem in the mood to tell her where they were headed. Other than 'hunting', he hadn't given her any more information. "And you think Serj will be okay with those men locked up so close to him?" Vicky had to shout to be heard over the wind.

"I've taken Flynn off his duty at the gym and asked him to watch their cells while we're out."

Vicky stopped. "You've done *what*?"

Unlike Vicky, Hugh continued to march up the overgrown and uneven hill. "The boy can look after a few cells, Vicky. Besides, all he needs to do is make sure Serj doesn't get to them."

After a jog to catch up, her new crossbow heavy on her back, Vicky said, "Yeah, he sure can, but I figured you might have consulted with me beforehand."

"What are you? His fucking mother or something?"

"How many times do I need to be reminded I'm not his mother? Were this world not the fuck up it's become, then I would be his legal guardian, and I would be entitled to make decisions on his behalf."

Completely disregarding Vicky's comments, Hugh continued to climb the seemingly never-ending hill with his long strides. "Besides, Flynn seems to understand Serj better than almost anyone I've met … apart from Jessica, of course. I think if anyone can talk him down, it'll be Flynn."

There seemed little point in making the same argument again. Hugh had made his decision and she couldn't do anything about it now. Vicky changed the subject. "You don't think the people of Home will be pissed that we've gone out, with everything that's going on?"

"We've come out hunting. When they're eating deer stew, I'm sure they'll be grateful for our little expedition." Hugh stopped this time, his tense shoulders raised when he turned to Vicky. "Look, last night was rough … for everyone. I can't stay trapped in that place today. I need to stretch my legs."

When they set off again, the long grass dragged on their progress. Were it not for the strong breeze, then the sound of their steps might have given them away. At present, only animals that stood downwind from them would be able to hear their approach. Sure, it made for hard going to walk with the wind in their faces, but it would pay off when they caught something.

"So if you've made your mind up already," Vicky said. "Why have the trial for the two men who we think killed Jessica?"

"There's no *think* about it. They *did* kill her."

"My question still stands."

"I suppose, like society before everything went to shit, we have to keep the people placated. Either that or fearful, and I'm not ready to use that form of manipulation yet."

"Yet? So you plan on using it?"

Hugh ignored her again. "If we give the people a trial of the two murdering bastards, it will keep them relaxed about the fact that they will get the same fair treatment should they ever have a charge levelled at them."

"But you're the judge, Hugh."

A shrug and Hugh's eyes smiled even if his face didn't. "That style of democracy worked for the longest time, I don't see why it won't continue to work. All that matters to the diners is how polished the table is, not the woodworm eating it from the inside. Keep them placated and we can run Home how we see fit."

"That seems like a very cynical way to look at things."

"I'm a realist, Vicky."

The man said it as if everything that came from his mouth was a fact. Vicky, on the other hand, felt like she needed to wade through his bullshit to find the occasional kernels of truth. "Have you ever had to deal with anything like this before?" Vicky said.

Hugh squinted into the wind, crow's feet running all the way to his temples.

The bitter chill ran so cold, it stung Vicky's eyes and drew a tear from them.

"I haven't had anything quite like this before," Hugh finally said. "Most of the evictions have been with people like the nutter you saw the other day. The people at Home are happy for me to make decisions in that situation."

"After you've kicked someone out of Home—"

"Evicted," Hugh said.

"Evicted. After you've evicted the people who need to go, has anyone ever come back?"

"No. It's why we sound the alarm. We need to make sure they don't survive."

"Then why don't you just kill them and make it easier?"

"Again, for the people of Home."

"Huh?"

"It's all about the ceremony. Also, it helps to remind the people that there are consequences should they step out of line."

Before Vicky could ask any more questions, Hugh reached the brow of a hill, lifted the binoculars he had around his neck and said, "This is where I wanted to bring you."

The final few feet of the climb burned Vicky's calf muscles.

Before she could comment, Hugh handed her his pair of binoculars. "I thought it was important that you came to see this."

The place stretched out as large as Home, but all above ground. Chain-link fences, barbed wire, a main large building—it looked like an old prison. "What is this place?" Vicky said.

"Meet the neighbours."

"How long have they been here?"

"Five years, maybe more."

"And you don't want to go and see them to try to link our communities?"

When Hugh pointed down to the place, he said, "Have a look in that far corner at the large building.

The courtyard—easily the size of the canteen in Home—had a long building in one corner. As Vicky scanned it, she gasped.

Next to the long building stood a row of chain-link fences and cages. They imprisoned what looked like hundreds of people. "What the fuck?"

"They don't look like the best people, do they?" Hugh said.

"We need to do something."

"Like what?"

"We need to let them know that they can't treat people that way."

Hugh threw his arm out to invite Vicky down the hill. "Go on, then, be my guest."

"There has to be a way to stop it. How can you live side by side with the fuckers and not want to do anything about it?"

"I didn't say I *don't* want to. I just don't think it's practical. We don't know how many people they have, but we do know how many we have, and it's not a war I'm confident we can win. So, for now, we have to let them go about their business. Maybe we'll be able to do something in the future."

While Hugh spoke, Vicky continued to look over the sprawling structure. Well fortified, it looked like it had no problem with keeping people in, or keeping people out.

"We've had a couple of search parties disappear in the past. Now, it's entirely likely that the parties strayed too far from Home and found themselves captured by this lot. But we have no proof of that, so we have to assume they were attacked by the diseased."

At the top of the hill—the wind rocking her on her heels—Vicky stared down at the fort and her jaw hung loose.

"I thought it was important I showed you where it is," Hugh said. "I want you to know where to avoid. If I've learned anything from our considerable lack of contact with one another, it's that these people are best left well alone. Besides, as much as I hate having them, our enemies are the diseased, not other communities."

With that, Hugh spun on his heel and strode back down the hill.

A lot of valid points, but none of them eased the nausea that sank through Vicky's guts. At some point, they might wish they'd done more about their brutal neighbours. Vicky followed Hugh down the hill back toward Home. Back to the trial. Back to conspire with him to convict two men of a murder she couldn't be sure they'd committed.

# Chapter Thirty-Seven

The only courtrooms Vicky had ever seen had been ridiculously dramatised versions used in reality TV programmes. Judge Julian, Judge James, Judge Julie … an absurd line-up of power-hungry, fame-hungry old codgers whose names started with the letter *J*. They lorded it over the accused, a parody of their profession as they slammed the gavel down and dealt their judgment.

Although, the one's Vicky had seen looked more professional than the makeshift attempt they'd thrown together in the canteen in Home. Enough chairs had been arranged for everyone in the facility to come to watch the proceedings. An aisle ran down the centre of the seats, dividing them equally. A look over the gathered crowd and Vicky's heart fluttered. Some of the seats sat empty, but not many. It seemed like most of Home had turned up. And why wouldn't they? They hardly had anything better to do.

A shake took a hold of Vicky as she walked up the aisle in the middle. The people turned to look at her, and a host of anxieties swirled through her mind. What if she couldn't get her words out? What if she had a panic attack? What if she threw up? What if the men didn't do it? The air felt harder to breathe, thinner almost. With each slow step forward, Vicky felt every eye in the room turn to her. Their collective stare dazzled her and she cleared her throat several times to remove the dryness from it. It had little effect.

Hugh and Serj didn't seem to agree on much, but they both seemed keen on Vicky being the one to put the case against the two accused men. As someone who hadn't been there that long, she had a level of impartiality the others didn't. When Flynn saw Vicky's nervous reaction to the suggestion, he put himself forward, but she couldn't allow that. Were it not a choice between her and Flynn, then she would have flat refused.

Joint judges for the case, Hugh and Serj sat behind a table at the head of the room and faced the crowd. The two defendants sat in the front row, awaiting their judgment. Fresh cable ties had been used to bind their wrists, which they rested on the table in front of them. They both looked like paler, sweatier versions of their already pale and sweaty selves.

The sheer amount of bodies in the canteen had raised the heat of the room, and sweat itched beneath Vicky's collar. By the time she'd arrived at the front, her shirt stuck to her neck. She nodded at Hugh and Serj, drew a deep breath of the cabbage-scented air, and turned to face the silenced crowd. Every pair of eyes stared at her, and for the briefest moment, she drew a blank. Then she looked at Flynn, who smiled brilliance her way. Without judgment or expectation, he'd clearly forgiven her failings and willed her on with a gentle nod of his head.

Vicky pointed at the two men. "We're here today to put

these two men on trial. Since the day they showed up, they've had a problem with Jessica. Then, as soon as they get let out of their cells, Jessica turns up dead."

A glance at both Serj and Hugh, and Vicky saw them wince at her directness. She kept her attention on Hugh. Something seemed off about the man, but if she couldn't prove what, then she had no case against him.

"We have a motive; when these two men arrived, they brought a bitten woman with them and tried to get her into Home. The woman would have turned into one of the diseased, so Jessica took on the unenviable task of executing her to protect the rest of us. Naturally, these men found this upsetting. Who wouldn't, right? I suppose the question is, did they find it upsetting enough to murder out of revenge for their dead friend?"

Out of breath and with her heart running away with her—the muted crowd all watching on—Vicky tried to force herself to slow down and breathe before she continued. "Jessica believed the men would understand her actions, even if it took them a while to get over the initial upset of it. Ever compassionate, she believed the men deserved to live among us while they managed their grief, so she took a chance on them. She let them out when we would have kept them in their cells for longer."

As silent as the rest of the room, the men at the front glared at Vicky. It added heat to Vicky's already flustered state, but she continued. "The night we found Jessica, she'd been stabbed. Although not dead, she'd been so badly wounded that she died a few minutes later. After a search of these men's rooms, we found a bloody knife and Jessica's necklace."

The taller man of the two—the blond one with the

bloodshot eyes and mess of thick hair—flinched at Vicky's words. Although he opened his mouth to speak, his friend got in there first.

"They found it in *his* room, not mine. I haven't done anything."

A hard frown and the blond man turned to his friend. "I didn't do anything *either*."

"I'm not saying you did. I can't defend you though, because all I know for sure is that *my* room was clear."

"So, ladies and gentlemen," Vicky said, "it would seem that not even his friend trusts him."

The blond man scowled at the man next to him.

"I don't have much more to say. I think I've given you the motive and the evidence linking at least one of these men to the murder. And now we have the second one ready to sell his mate up the river if it means he can walk away. Personally, I don't trust either of them. I'm appealing to you because you have the say. Beneath each of your seats is a piece of red card and a piece of green card. If you want these men to be evicted from Home, raise your red cards. If you think they should stay and live among us, then it's green."

It took about five seconds for a sea of red to meet Vicky's question. Relieved at the court case being over, Vicky breathed more easily. However, she couldn't shake the nagging feeling that these men were innocent. When she turned to Hugh and Serj, the men nodded at her. She'd done a good job. Well, she'd made sure it went as they'd hoped it would at least.

Hugh and Serj then walked over to the two men and forced them to their feet.

Once Hugh had pulled the tall, blond man up, he addressed the crowd. "Thank you for your time and input. We value democracy in Home and we wanted to be sure you had your say as to how we dealt with these men. After all, them being here puts all of our safety at risk. We plan to evict them immediately."

Nausea turned in Vicky's stomach as she watched Hugh. Had she done the right thing?

# Chapter Thirty-Eight

It shouldn't have been a surprise how things panned out in the courtroom. Hugh had pretty much given Vicky a blow-by-blow plan as to how it would go. But as Vicky stood next to Hugh, Serj, Flynn, and the two convicted men, a deep sense of dread sank through her. The so-called democracy they'd claimed to have in Home had been a farce. What if Vicky found herself on the wrong end of Home's democracy in the future?

Exhausted from her part in the courtroom, Vicky looked at the two 'guilty' men. They stood before the exit to Home, their wrists still cable tied. Neither man spoke. Instead, they seemed lost in their own resignation. Both of them—pale-faced and with pursed lips—stared straight ahead, refusing to acknowledge the bustling crowd crammed in behind them.

Both Hugh and Serj shared a look with one another before Hugh nodded. At his acknowledgement, Flynn stepped forward and undid the bolts on the large door. Despite the sheer weight of people, the snapping of the locks cracked through the place as if it were silent. Like the gavel they didn't have, the two heavy knocks sentenced the men to their deaths.

When Flynn opened the door, the fresh breeze came in. Vicky usually found it invigorating to inhale the grassy scent, but today it had been tinged with the bitterness of guilt—guilt, if nothing else, at the fact that these men didn't get a fair trial.

The reluctant men needed a shove from Hugh and Serj to get them outside. Once they had crossed Home's threshold, they stared out into the field of long grass in front of them.

After Flynn had closed the door and slipped the two bolts back into place, Hugh faced the crowd.

Instead of watching him, Vicky watched the two men. Not only did they continue to stare straight ahead, but they didn't look at one another either. Side by side, they seemed alone in their contemplation of their own demise. They couldn't even find comfort in a fellow exile.

Unable to hear his words as Hugh put a show on for the gathered crowd, Vicky found herself stuck on the same thought. *What if they've got it wrong? What if the men are innocent?*

The wailing noise of the siren snapped Vicky from her daze. She looked over at Hugh, who stepped away from the button to go to the window on the other side of the door. A dark and mirthful grimace twisted his features and something close to enjoyment drenched his sadistic leer.

The two men stumbled forward into the long grass. Each one walked with his head held high. Each one walked slowly. They couldn't choose whether they lived or died, but both of them could choose how they met their end. Dignified in their death, they faced the screaming horde of diseased that came into view.

As Vicky watched on, a lump swelled in her throat. She

didn't see two murderers; she saw two men who'd survived in a world they had no right to survive in.

The men fell at virtually the same time as the pack of diseased split and took one down each. Erect and proud, both men fell like cardboard cutouts and vanished into the long grass beneath the swarm of bodies on top of them.

When Vicky saw the first of the diseased pull its head back—blood dripping from its maw—she looked away and moved to one side.

The space she left got filled by one of the onlookers.

Flynn came to Vicky's side, his face pale. "Whether they did it or not," he said, "it's a shit way to go."

"And you know what," Vicky said, "we never even asked them their names. They came to this place and we caged them like animals. Now we're putting them down like animals."

# Chapter Thirty-Nine

After they'd sent the two men to their deaths, Hugh had told Vicky to take the rest of the day off. Too exhausted to visit the gym, Vicky wandered until she ended up outside the room they'd found Jessica's body in. As she stood in the corridor, anxiety ate away at her like acid. There had to be more to Jessica's death.

The room had been cordoned off, but Vicky slipped through the tape and flicked the light on. A bloodstain remained on the floor. Someone would have to clean it up; someone not as close to Jessica as any of the Home guards were. She'd speak to Piotr when she had time. A practical man, he seemed to have a level enough head to deal with it. He also didn't have the connection to Jessica that the rest of them did.

An empty storeroom, it seemed like a strange location for Jessica to be murdered in. How did they get her there in the first place? And if they killed her somewhere else, how did they transport the body without getting noticed? Although, late at night Home didn't see much activity, so moving a dead body around might not have been as hard as it would seem. But then there would have been the blood. She must have been murdered in the empty room. No way could someone have moved her without leaving a trail. She'd been stabbed more times than a pincushion.

A hunch and nothing more, Vicky had to follow it through. She headed toward Hugh's bedroom.

On her way, Vicky passed the gym. The slamming of feet against the treadmill called out into the corridor. When she peered inside, she saw Hugh red-faced and running with everything he had. Vicky stepped into the stagnant air in the hot room and stood beside Hugh's bag. Just out of his line of sight, she made it look like she planned to get on the treadmill. As she leaned down to tie up her trainers, she reached into Hugh's bag and pulled out his room key. Unlike the massive key ring he had for everywhere else, Hugh kept the one for his room separate. Vicky coughed to hide the gentle tinkle it made.

When she stood up again, she said, "Will you be here long? I want to go to the loo and then come to run with you."

Too gassed from his run, Hugh nodded at her, and Vicky gave him a thumbs-up as she left.

Once she'd stepped out of Hugh's line of sight, she took off, sprinting down the corridor to his room while he remained in the gym.

\*\*\*

Out of breath from the run, Vicky stopped outside Hugh's bedroom, looked both ways, and slipped the key into the lock. The key spun until the lock released. Another quick look up and down the corridor and finding it still remained clear, Vicky opened the door and slipped inside.

The second she'd entered the room, Vicky saw the corner of a white sheet beneath Hugh's bed. It had bloodstains on it, lots of fucking bloodstains. She already shook with adrenaline, so when she saw the sheets, she shivered beyond control and whispered, "Fuck." That must have been how he transported her body to the storeroom. It made sense that he thought he could sit on the evidence too. After all, who watched the watchmen?

Vicky knelt down and peered beneath Hugh's bed. Next to the stuffed sheets sat the small black walking boots that Jessica always wore. The air left Vicky's body in a gasp and nausea flipped her stomach. She knew the two men were innocent. The case had been too convenient. The way Hugh engineered the men's exile reeked of wrongdoing. The leering sneer on his face like the devil lurked beneath his skin as he pressed the siren to call the diseased to them. The man smelled guilty, and now she'd put the pieces together, Vicky could see he positively reeked of it. After she drew a stuttered breath, she muttered again, "Fuck."

Another rush of adrenaline sent Vicky's pulse ragged and her head spun. She quickly stood up and left Hugh's room. The corridor remained empty, so she clicked the lock shut and made her way back to the gym.

\*\*\*

It would have looked suspicious had Vicky not returned to the gym, so she got back to Hugh as quickly as she could. Next to the treadmill, just out of his line of sight again, she adjusted her shoes for a second time and slipped the key back in his bag.

When she stepped onto the treadmill next to the man, her head still spinning, she cranked the setting up to seven. At a fast walk, she had no more in her tired legs.

When Hugh turned his speed up next to her, she felt his silent challenge, but Vicky didn't respond.

"What's the matter?" Hugh asked. "You not feeling up to it today?"

A shake of her head and Vicky couldn't find the words. She then hit the large red button on the treadmill and stepped off it. "I'm sorry. This whole Jessica thing has done my head in. I need to go and rest."

Without looking at Hugh, she hurried to the doorway and said one last, "Sorry," as she walked out.

## Chapter Forty

No matter how clean he appeared, Vicky couldn't escape the fact that she shared her tiny personal space with a teenage boy. When she returned to their room, his stale smell hung as a combination of sweat and flatulence.

Flynn lay back, oblivious to his festering pit.

Vicky sat down on her bed and the flimsy cot creaked beneath her weight. Although she felt Flynn's eyes on her, she didn't look back at him. Instead, she rested her elbows on her knees, dropped her head into her hands, and stared at the blue linoleum floor.

"What's up?" Flynn asked.

But she didn't reply. The past twenty minutes swirled as a confused mess through her mind, and the words to express it existed just out of her reach.

After a few seconds of silence, Flynn's bed groaned from where he sat up. The small walkway between the two beds stretched just wide enough for Vicky's knees to nearly touch Flynn's bed on the other side. So when Flynn sat up too, his long legs bridged the gap and rested against Vicky. She shifted away from him.

"What's going on, Vicky?"

"I've had a rough day. It's been long. I dunno, seeing those men taken out. It just—"

"But they *killed* Jessica," Flynn interrupted.

"That's certainly what they got accused of."

A moment's silence and Flynn said for a second time, "What's going on?"

The tears she'd held back since she'd first seen Jessica's dead body rushed forward in a hot wave. Within seconds, they'd soaked her cheeks and she stuttered when she tried to draw a breath. A few more deep inhales and she levelled out a little before she looked up at Flynn.

He regarded her with a confused frown as he looked from one of her eyes to the other and Vicky broke down again. "I'm not sure they did it, Flynn."

Flynn gasped. "Who else could have done it?"

"I snuck into Hugh's room while he worked out in the gym and found bloody sheets and Jessica's shoes beneath his bed. Now I'm not saying *he* did it, but those sheets could have been wrapped around Jessica's bleeding body when he dragged her down to the empty storeroom."

"That's ridiculous," Flynn said. "Why would Hugh do it?"

"I don't know, and I'm not sure he did do it, but *he* was the one who found the knife and necklace in the man's room. *He* made the process of evicting them run as quickly and smoothly as it did. *He* steered a decision towards convicting them. I got behind that because I couldn't find any evidence to the contrary."

"You suspected him from the start?"

"Do you trust him?"

Flynn didn't answer.

"When I saw the look on Hugh's face as the men walked away from Home … and the body language of the men. I dunno … I just don't think they were guilty."

With a deep exhale that puffed his cheeks out, Flynn ran his hand through his hair and shook his head. "I'm sure there are a lot of things Hugh doesn't tell us, but murdering Jessica?"

"I don't think you'd question it if you'd have seen his room."

"But why would he do it?" Flynn asked again.

"That's the thing. I don't know. It doesn't make sense."

"We should tell Serj."

"No!"

Flynn pulled his head back at Vicky's outburst.

"Serj is too emotionally involved in this. If we tell him, there'll be chaos."

"But I'd feel terrible if Serj found out that I knew and hadn't told him."

"We need to be sure first, Flynn. We have to work out what's going on before we tell *anyone*."

The springs on Flynn's bed creaked again as he shifted around on it. "What if Hugh kills more people? By the time we're sure, he will have gotten rid of the sheets and Jessica's shoes."

"What if I've got it wrong?" Vicky said. "You've seen how they evict people from this place. I'm not going to let that happen to you."

Silence descended on the small room again. After she'd kicked her shoes off her tired feet, Vicky lay back on her bed and stared up at the white ceiling.

"Then we should leave," Flynn said.

"And leave all of these innocent people behind? Leave Serj and Piotr and all of the others in this place? They're good people. We shouldn't shun them because of one bad egg."

"One bad *murdering* egg," Flynn said. "So what do we do, then?"

"I think we need to play it smart," Vicky said as she continued to stare up at the ceiling. "I need to build a case against Hugh so when it comes to presenting it to the community, we can sentence him without any fear of being wrong."

"How long will that take?"

"I don't know, Flynn. I don't know."

# Chapter Forty-One

Vicky clenched her teeth against the biting wind. Maybe no windier than usual, but since she'd spent so much time underground, the elements had more of an impact on her when she stepped out into them. A look across the long swaying grass and Vicky's eyes burned. She'd had a restless night's sleep, her mind on spin dry as she tried to put all the pieces together. Not even the fresh smell of nature could lift her spirit.

Although Vicky scanned their environment, pretending to look for the diseased or something to hunt, she kept her eye on Hugh in her peripheral vision. Her finger rested on the trigger of her crossbow. If he gave her half an excuse, she'd sink a bolt into his chest.

The pair had said little to one another while they walked, so when Hugh spoke, it ran an extra twist of tension through Vicky. "Do you think we'll see the men who killed Jessica?"

The intensity of his stare made Vicky uncomfortable, and heat flushed her cheeks. She stalled for a moment before she finally said, "I hope not. It felt bad enough kicking them out yesterday; I don't want to see them now they've turned."

A bitter scowl as he looked out over the landscape again, and Hugh lowered his voice to a growl. "They deserved everything they got."

They might have walked side by side, but Hugh clearly led the way as he guided them back to the spot they'd been to the other day: the spot that overlooked the prison-like community.

Because Vicky didn't respond, Hugh shot her an aggressive, "Don't they?"

A gentle squeeze on the crossbow's trigger and Vicky shrugged. "If they did it."

"What's *that* supposed to mean?"

"What if someone set them up?"

Impatience ran through Hugh's words and the air between them thickened. The atmosphere felt loaded like they were moments away from a thunderstorm. An almighty power sat coiled in Hugh's large and tense form, ready to be sparked into action at any moment. "Who would set them up?" he said. "And how? How did they manage to get the bloody knife and Jessica's necklace into their room before I got there? It would have been impossible."

The aggression in Hugh's delivery backed Vicky into a corner. His bullying might have been delivered as questions, but he didn't want answers. So Vicky said nothing in response to him; instead, she continued to look around as they walked up the hill toward their neighbouring community. "Do you think we'll find any animals today?"

"You think you've already found one, don't you? You think you're so fucking smart."

When Vicky turned to Hugh, she saw he'd raised his

crossbow and pointed it straight at her. "Now put your fucking weapon on the ground."

A dry gulp and Vicky did as he said. She saw the same darkness in his eyes that she'd seen when he'd watched the men leave Home. "Why did you do it, Hugh?"

"Keep walking," Hugh said as he forced her up the hill.

When they got to the top, the wind stronger than ever, Hugh said, "Look at it."

Vicky did as he said. It looked like a prison from a developing nation. Erected on a shoestring budget and built with little concern for the prisoners, it had just one purpose—keep people contained, comfort and human rights be damned.

"You don't realise how lucky you were. Home is paradise compared to a lot of the places around here. You've been to the mall; you can see how people are treated down there. But you know what, I think we're too fucking nice at Home. You helped me see that."

"Huh?"

"Well, you and Flynn. When you two arrived and you were more useful to me than ninety-five percent of the people already in Home, I realised that I'd been mugged off for years. I work like an arsehole so those freeloaders can have a nice, cushy life."

"But that's why you decided to make them train in the gym, right?"

"That was too little, too late. Food's running out at Home, Vicky. For some reason, the farm can't produce the quantities it once did, and those lazy fucks are eating it all. I don't want to starve looking after those fat losers."

"So why kill Jessica?"

The directness of her question seemed to knock Hugh off guard, his eyes narrowing as he stared at her. "Because I wanted to kick a lot of the people out of Home and she thought I was wrong to do it. She thought we could find another way and she threatened to tell everyone what I was doing."

"So you killed her?"

"Yep. We were fucking, Jessica and I, did you know that?"

The grief between Serj and Hugh flicked through Vicky's mind. "That's why Serj hates you."

"I'd assume so. Not that he knows, but he must have had a hunch. I mean, as much as he pretended he didn't know, he knew."

A gargoyle grin split Hugh's face. "Did you seriously think I didn't see you steal the key from my bag the other day? Had you been a bit more savvy with it, then maybe you wouldn't be here now."

The hill that led down to the neighbouring community ran steep. Vicky rocked in the strong wind as she looked to the bottom. The strength drained from her legs and her stomach lurched.

As Hugh shouldered the crossbow and closed one eye to peer down the sight, he said, "Jessica wanted to break it off with me. That's why I told her about my plans to kick people out. I wanted to confide in her. I thought the trust might make her want to stay. But she didn't."

"I used to think you were strong," Vicky said. "Then I saw how you reacted to being chased by the diseased. And now this: killing innocent people."

"*Innocent*? Jessica was about to sell me up the river to the people of Home." Hugh pointed at his chest. "*My community* and *she* was going against me. I can't allow that."

When Vicky saw the slight twitch of his finger on the trigger, she dropped to the ground. The *whoosh* of the bolt ran over her head as she grabbed a handful of dirt and launched it at Hugh. Enough to cause a distraction, she rolled away from him down the steep hill.

Within seconds, gravity had taken a hold of Vicky and accelerated her escape. As she rolled and bounced on the lumpy ground, each jolt stung and drove more of the wind from her body. With every revolution, she caught sight of Hugh at the top of the hill and heard another *whoosh* as another bolt narrowly missed her.

Her back crashed against a particularly large lump on the ground and drove the rest of the wind from Vicky's body in a deep bark. Her diaphragm spasmed as she continued toward the prison at the bottom.

The sound of the bolts ceased. Hugh had fired maybe four or five at her and missed with each one. Maybe she'd get away. But instead of a bolt, the fizz and pink smoke of a flare shot over her head. Then another one followed it almost immediately afterwards.

When Vicky hit the fence for their neighbouring community at the bottom, it ran a shaking rattle away from her in both directions. Battered from the fall, she lay immobile on the ground and gasped for breath. Every part of her body ached. The two flares that Hugh had fired billowed smoke around her, and it made it hard for her to see up the hill. As she squinted up through the pink haze, the wind blew a gap in it. It gave her the time to see the figure of Hugh stare down at her for a few more seconds before he turned and walked away.

What had he seen? Why didn't he try to kill her?

Before Vicky could think on it any further, three large men and one woman appeared over her. One of the men—small with sharp features and greasy black hair—grinned down at her. He looked like a rat. "Well, well, well, look what Home have delivered to us."

The other three laughed as they closed their ring around Vicky.

The biggest of the three men then raised his fist and drove a heavy blow into the centre of Vicky's face.

The first punch spun Vicky out and threw stars across her vision, but she remained conscious. Sharp and stinging pain made her eyes water. Blood ran into her mouth from what must have been a broken nose. The figures above her turned into blurred blobs, and before Vicky could react, one of the blobs hit her again and her world went dark.

## Chapter Forty-Two

Vicky opened her eyes to a deep sting that stretched through her face. When she wriggled her nose, she winced at the jarring pain of it. It felt like her sinuses had been packed with crushed glass. Once she sat up, the pulse of her headache compressed her skull, and although she clamped a hand to either side of her head, she couldn't ease the pain.

Vicky blinked several times to try to clear her vision and looked at her surroundings. A small square cell about four paces by four paces, it had walls made from chain-link fence and a concrete floor. Other than Vicky, the cold cell stood empty

Despite the swollen mess that clogged her nose, it didn't take away the reek of piss and shit. Vicky retched several times at the stink of it. She'd obviously been imprisoned by the people of the community at the bottom of the hill, but what the fuck did they want with her?

The cell next to Vicky's backed up against a brick wall the same as hers did. Easily twenty paces by twenty paces, Vicky's cell would fit in it four to five times over. It currently sat empty.

Hard to tell from her current position, but the long wall

must have been the back of the building she'd seen when she'd looked at the place from the top of the hill. A small alleyway ran down past her cell. It probably led to the front of the building, but Vicky couldn't see clearly enough from her current position to be sure.

A wide open forecourt stretched between Vicky's cell and the main gate to the place. It had the same rough concrete ground that Vicky currently sat on. It also had two manhole covers in it. Despite the darkness of night, she saw scratches in the ground surrounding the holes. It looked like the covers were removed regularly.

As Vicky searched the darkness beyond the complex, she looked in the direction of Home. Not that she could see much. The communities stood close to one another. So close, yet they existed in two separate worlds. High-end technology on one side, and medieval barbarism on the other.

Before Vicky could take in any more of her surroundings, a shrill *peep* of a whistle pulled her attention to the front gate. A man and a woman appeared from the darkness. Both wore hoodies that hid their faces, and each carried a bloodstained machete. Another blow of his whistle and the man banged the handle of his large blade against the bars of the gate. The entire chain-link fence rattled from the contact. "Come on, Moira, let us in."

He had an accent Vicky couldn't place. Australian? South African? She couldn't tell.

A woman with two hulking men appeared along the walkway that ran next to Vicky's cell. Despite her curiosity, Vicky cowered away from them and stared at the ground as they passed. Once they'd stepped into the forecourt, she watched them from the corner of her eye.

Older than Vicky by maybe ten years, the woman had wild black hair, sharp features pulled tight with bitterness, and she wore a long white fur coat. The large men by her side both carried battleaxes and marched in perfect time with her wide, flourishing strides. The rim of the woman's coat billowed out like a bell.

When the three of them got to the gate, the woman—who Vicky assumed to be Moira—opened it. The man and woman stepped in. They kept their hoods up so Vicky still couldn't see their faces. The woman had a grip on a long chain, which she tugged with her as she stepped through the gate. Because of the darkness, Vicky hadn't seen the shackled people until now, and she drew a sharp involuntary breath as the first of them were led through.

Not quite sure how many prisoners they had, Vicky watched on with her stomach in her throat. Each slave dragged their feet as they were pulled forward; the chain was attached to large metal collars clamped around their necks. They all had sunken eyes with deep bags beneath them and were so skinny they looked like they could snap.

The first of the chained people—a boy of no more than about eighteen—carried a brown sack with him. From what Vicky could see, they all had one. The boy emptied his out and three diseased heads hit the hard ground like spilled coconuts.

One of Moira's guards went to the manhole cover closest to him and lifted it up. The heavy metal object scraped over the ground as he dragged it away. He then kicked the three heads down into it.

The boy stood at the front of the line, shaking as he watched Moira, the whites of his eyes stark in his dirty face. When Moira nodded at him, the hooded man with the machete undid the collar on his neck, and the second of Moira's guards opened the cage next to Vicky. They led the boy in.

A man was next in line. He stepped forward and emptied his sack. His had four diseased heads in it, each one thudding as they hit the hard ground.

Moira nodded, so the man with the machete freed him and led him to be with the boy in the cage. The next eight people repeated the process. Men, women, and older children, each one had at least three heads in their respective bags, and each one looked nervous as they awaited Moira's approval of their haul.

When they came to a girl no older than Flynn, Vicky's heart sank. Whatever she had in her sack, from the way she shook, shivered, and cried, she clearly didn't have what Moira would deem appropriate. She upended the brown sack and just one head fell out.

Moira looked down at it for a few seconds, the scowl on her angular face locking in a demonic glare. She then closed her eyes and drew a deep breath. It seemed to still her rage, because when she looked back at the girl, a calm had settled over her features.

The girl shook her head. "No, please, Moira, no. Please. I tried as hard as I could."

After Moira's personal guard had kicked the girl's offering down the manhole, he walked over to her.

"Please, anything but that. Please."

The hooded man with the machete undid the girl's collar and the girl's wail echoed through the forecourt.

It rang so shrilly it hurt Vicky's ears.

"Please!"

Before Moira's guard could drag the girl away, Moira raised a hand to stop him. She walked over to the girl and grabbed her face in a pinch, which forced a pout from her. So close their noses nearly touched, Moira smiled. "Now, I consider myself to be a fair master, and I don't think it would be fair if you didn't get the same punishment as everyone else, do you?"

The shackled people in the line behind the girl all winced as they watched the drama unfold in front of them.

Whatever would happen next, the tension made Vicky feel sick to her stomach.

"How do you think the others would feel if I went easy on you, eh? What would they do to you if I let you join them in the cage after I've punished them in the past?"

The girl didn't answer any of the questions. A skinny thing, she pulled away from Moira, stared down at the ground, and cried to the point where snot ran from her nose. She shook like she had hypothermia.

Speaking in no more than a whisper, Moira said, "It wouldn't be fair now, would it? You know the rules: three diseased heads or a night in the hole."

At that moment, the girl's legs gave way beneath her and she fell to the ground in a broken heap.

A few seconds passed where Vicky could only hear the girl's sobs. Moira then shook her head and spat at the girl. "Pathetic." She turned to her guard. "Take her away."

The guard dragged the girl toward the open manhole by her hair. The girl twisted and screamed, but she couldn't halt their progress. He then grabbed her beneath her arms, lifted her from the ground, and dropped her into the hole he'd been kicking the severed heads down.

The girl's scream dropped into the tight space with her and Vicky's entire body writhed with fear and revulsion.

# Chapter Forty-Three

The girl's screams and cries called from the hole as the rest of the line emptied their sacks. When it got to just three people left, Vicky froze to see the man from Home. The one from the farm. The one Hugh had asked Piotr and the other farm worker to take away. Hugh must have evicted him, and he must have survived because Vicky hadn't heard the alarm. A covert eviction, Hugh couldn't have afforded to make a fuss with it; otherwise people would have found out.

Only a few days since she'd seen him last, he now looked like one of the prisoners. Sallow cheeks, lank and greasy hair, hollow eyes …

When he looked up and made eye contact with Vicky, she suddenly realised she'd stared at him with her mouth agape. A flash of recognition shimmered across his eyes, but it vanished as he emptied his bag and focused on Moira. Three heads fell to the ground. After Moira looked at the heads, she nodded and he joined the others in the cell.

Although the man glanced at Vicky again as he crossed the courtyard, he didn't reveal he knew her. The spark of familiarity had been enough. No doubt they'd talk later.

Moira's guard grinned as he kicked one of the new heads down the hole.

"Just stop it, please?" the girl called up at him, her voice echoing in what sounded like a cramped pit down below.

The guard's smile widened and he kicked the other two down on top of her.

A woman, close to Moira's age—late forties to early fifties—brought up the rear of the line. Before she'd even had a chance to speak, Vicky saw she had an empty sack. Tears ran down her face and her entire frame sagged with defeat.

Moira stared at her and then at her sack. After a deep breath, she shook her head. "Ashley, Ashley, Ashley, what are we going to do with you?"

Although Ashley opened her mouth to reply, Moira cut her off with a raised hand. "Don't answer that. We all know what we're going to do with you."

The guard by the manhole with the heads in it slid the heavy metal cover across, dampening the girl's scream inside and no doubt casting her into complete darkness. He then walked to the other manhole cover and dragged it free.

Ashley watched on, her grey hair a chaotic bird's nest, her wide eyes frantic as she continued to cry. It seemed that everyone—even the guards—held their breath. Everyone except Moira, who bounced on the balls of her feet, seemingly struggling to contain her glee.

The sound from the second hole drowned out the girl in the first. It sent a chill through Vicky and the hairs lifted on the back of her neck. Shifting to find more comfort on the cold and hard floor, Vicky listened to the calls of several diseased rising up into the night.

"This is the third time now, Ashley," Moira said. "You know the rules; three strikes and you're out."

Something broke in Ashley at that moment. Where Vicky had expected her to scream and cry, the woman's body went stiff instead and she shook. She appeared to be fitting.

Moira looked down at Ashley's crotch and said, "Fucking hell, love, have you just pissed yourself?"

But Ashley didn't reply, her wide glazed eyes showing she'd gotten lost in the chaos of her fear.

The hooded man with the machete undid Ashley's collar and grabbed her scrawny arm. He then led her to the guard at the second manhole.

"I'm true to my word," Moira said as her other guard locked the rest of the prisoners in the large cell. About twenty people in total, they didn't make a sound as they watched the drama play out in front of them. "When I say you get three strikes and you're out, I mean it. Three heads, that's the rule. You bring three heads back to me and you get to go back into the cage. If you're not good enough for the death of three diseased, then you're not good enough to live." Moira walked over to the first hole with the cover now replaced. She stamped on it. It sent out a loud *boom* and Vicky heard the faint cry from the girl they'd locked in there. "I go easy on you for the first two strikes, but if the hole isn't enough to inspire you to do better, then there's just no helping you, I'm afraid."

Moira stopped talking as she watched Ashley get dragged over to the open manhole where the diseased screams came out of. The dishevelled prisoner walked as if on autopilot and stared into space, her face slack, her eyes wide.

The guard looked at Moira when he reached the hole. Moira nodded and Vicky's stomach flipped to see the guard shove Ashley into it.

A *thud* sounded out as Ashley landed. It stirred up the roars of what sounded to be at least ten diseased in the pit, and Ashley finally screamed.

A wide smile spread across Moira's haggard face.

Ashley's screams stopped a few seconds later, replaced with a choked gargle.

The guard with the battleaxe slid the manhole cover back across the hole. The woman in the hoodie went to the front gate and locked it with a heavy padlock. The four guards and Moira then left the forecourt. They walked back past Vicky's cage and Vicky once more recoiled at their proximity.

Just before they'd gone from view, Vicky looked up and her heart damn near stopped when she met Moira's cold glare. Dark eyes, as dark as the night that surrounded them, stared straight into Vicky, but she said nothing. Moira clearly had plans for her.

The guards and Moira then disappeared into the rest of the complex.

With a numb arse from being sat on the ground for the entire time, Vicky got to her feet and paced her cell. The prisoners next to her watched her, especially the man from Home, but Vicky didn't look back. Instead, she looked out in the direction of the hilltop where Hugh had pushed her down. Only a few hours ago, she'd been safe up there. She should have seen it coming. She should have done more.

Before she could stop herself, a hot rush bucked through Vicky and she vomited on the floor of her cell. The sharp acidic kick of bile caught in her throat, suffocating her. A seal-like bark as she fought for breath and Vicky vomited again. The thick surge of half-digested food exploded from her and splashed on the floor. It cleared her airways and she could breathe again.

Using her sleeve to wipe her mouth, Vicky looked back up at the hilltop. Although dark, her eyes had adjusted a little and she saw something. She had to squint to be sure, but it certainly looked like the silhouette of a person on the ridge. Her heart skipped when she joined the dots and she spoke beneath her breath. "Flynn?"

# Chapter Forty-Four

The sound of a loud bell clattered through the courtyard. So loud, it riled the diseased in the pit below them and Vicky heard their roars through the ground beneath her feet.

For the past hour or so, Vicky had paced her small cell. The cold concrete ground turned her arse numb and gave her sore body no comfort. The swelling in her face throbbed worse than ever, her eyes sore and her nose clogged with the reek of sick and blood.

A dragging sound of wood over the rough concrete came down the walkway next to Vicky's cell before she saw anything. A few seconds later another guard that she hadn't seen before appeared. He had a huge barrel behind him. Despite the poor light, Vicky saw the contents of the barrel and her stomach lifted in a dry heave. The smell of rot—worse than even the diseased—walked past with him.

Vegetable peelings and animal bones … she even saw a used sanitary towel. How they still had them after a decade …

The man dragged the rotting, bloody, and raw mess around to the front of the large cage. The twenty or so people in the cage all moved to the back. They'd done this before and knew the drill.

When the man stopped outside, he rang his bell again and a tattoo of footsteps came from the direction of the walkway.

A few seconds later seven guards—three men and four women—all appeared by the man with the food. They all carried weapons. Bats, blades, and sticks. Not that they'd need to use them. The people in the cage next to Vicky had no spirit for a fight.

The man with the food opened the padlock on the cage's door. He then dragged the bucket of swill just inside before he walked out again, closed it behind him, and locked the lock.

The hungry eyes of the prisoners stared from sunken sockets at the food in front of them. It seemed impossible that they would eat from the bucket, but Vicky had never been so hungry she'd even consider it. She couldn't comprehend their desperation.

Once all the guards had vanished from sight, one of the prisoners stepped forward and turned to the group. The group had been silent since they'd been caged until now.

"Whose turn is it to eat first?" the man asked.

A boy of no more than about fourteen stepped forward and walked over to the barrel.

After a few minutes, he pulled a lump of old carrot out and half a raw potato. Clutching the food to his chest, he walked over to a corner of the cage and bit into the potato as if eating an apple.

Slack with shock, Vicky's jaw fell loose as she watched the next person walk up to the barrel.

The guy from Home and Vicky had looked at one another

several times. Although recognition passed between them, the man hadn't approached her yet. After several of the people had taken their food, Vicky watched the man shuffle over to the barrel.

Vicky checked the hill again. She'd checked frequently since she'd seen Flynn's silhouette, but she hadn't seen anything since. Hopefully he hadn't run into trouble out there. For his sake and for hers.

# Chapter Forty-Five

Half of the bucket, if not more, remained untouched. The used sanitary pad sat on top of the swill. The crowd had been careful to pick around it.

Although it had been dark for a few hours, it had taken until now for the stillness of night to settle over the place. The only sound Vicky heard came from the agitated diseased in the pit beneath them. The restless groans of discontent murmured through the ground like shocks after an earthquake.

Now it had gotten darker and quieter, the prisoners in the cage next to Vicky walked over to the corner farthest away from her. No dignity left, they took turns in emptying their bowels in full view of the others. The splutters of diarrhoea and slight moans of pain joined the murmurs from the diseased. The occasional strong gust of wind threw the cloying stench of viral shit Vicky's way.

When Vicky heard the hiss of a person in the cell next to her, she looked up. The cloak of night hid his dark features, but she knew it to be the man from the farm. A quick glance around to check there were no guards lurking in the shadows and Vicky sidled over to him.

When she got close, the man spoke in a whisper. "Hugh fucked you over too, huh?"

Vicky sighed. "Looks that way, doesn't it?"

"What was it? You found out how little food we had at Home?"

"Actually, he told me about the food crisis just before he shoved me down the hill toward this place. I found out he'd killed Jessica."

The man gasped.

"He had plans to kick a lot of people out of Home because we couldn't feed them, and Jessica didn't agree with that. He ended up killing her."

Silence hung for a second before the man said, "I had him as a coward and obviously saw how easily he banished people from Home, but I never had him as a cold-blooded murderer."

"He and Jessica were having a thing behind Serj's back. Not only did she disagree with him about kicking people out, but she also wanted to end it. Hugh's a man on the edge, and I think it pushed him over.

"How long have you been here?" Vicky asked.

"Three to four days. They captured me almost as soon as Hugh kicked me out." He sighed and looked at the ground. "If only I'd have turned left out of Home instead of right." When he looked back up, desperation sat in his bloodshot eyes. "We don't last long in this place. If food poisoning doesn't kill us, the lack of diseased we catch does. I've seen three people dropped into the pit in the short time I've been here. And seven more in the hole."

"And there's no way out?"

"Not that I've seen. Unless you have someone on the outside, you ain't getting out of here. They put you in your cell on your own for the first night, and then fold you into the group. By tomorrow you'll have a chain around your neck while you hunt the diseased."

Vicky almost told the man about Flynn. As a former member of Home, she felt like she owed him that. But if Flynn were to break her out, he'd need surprise on his side. The more people that knew about him, the lower his chances of success. "Why do you hunt the diseased?"

"Moira reckons we can thin their numbers. At least, that's what she says to us. I think it's just a creative way for her to torture people."

Vicky chewed on the inside of her mouth and looked out into the darkness for Flynn. "How many guards are there here?"

"I reckon about fifty."

"*Fifty?*"

"Yep. At least."

Before Vicky could reply, she caught movement in the shadows outside of the complex. "Thanks for the information. I'm going to do everything I can to escape from here. If I get out, I promise I'll come back for you, okay?"

The man fixed Vicky with a hard stare before he nodded and shuffled away from her.

Back in the middle of her cell, Vicky drew a deep breath and watched the space she'd seen movement in. When she squinted, she saw Flynn's form hunched down next to a bush right by the front gate. He held onto a rock so large he had to use both hands to lift it. When he saw that Vicky had seen him, he nodded at her and she nodded back.

Flynn then stood up and moved toward the gate, the rock above his head ready to smash into the lock.

A deep breath to still her frantic heart and Vicky readied herself to run.

# Chapter Forty-Six

The loud *crash* as Flynn brought the rock down on the padlock no doubt sent an alarm call to the guards, wherever they were.

Seconds later, the same bell Vicky had heard when they'd brought the food out rang through the place, frantic in its jangling rattle and backed up by a man screaming at the top of his voice. Vicky bounced on her toes, desperate to get free from her cage.

As Flynn shoved the front gate wide, Vicky listened to the sound of the guards gathering in the complex behind her.

Doors opened and slammed shut, and as Vicky watched Flynn run at her cage, she listened to the guard's heavy footfalls from where a considerable amount of them had clearly mobilised and headed their way.

In the moment it took Flynn to cross the forecourt, Vicky turned to the man from the farm and pushed her hands together as if to pray for his forgiveness. "I'll come back for you, I promise." He stared back at her, his face lank with shock.

Flynn got to Vicky's cell door and brought the rock down with another loud *crash* that shook the entire cell. He then cast the rock aside and ripped the door open for her.

The guards still hadn't appeared, but as Vicky ran from the cell out into the courtyard, she heard them call to one another.

Without looking back, she followed Flynn through the open front gate.

The desire to help the other prisoners dragged on her escape like she had a heavy tyre strapped to her, but she didn't stop. She couldn't. Not if she wanted to live.

As she ran near to the manhole covers, the thought of the young girl in the dark hole beneath her sent sharp shards of grief through her chest, but she kept going.

Once she'd run through the gates of the complex, Vicky followed Flynn up the hill away from the place. The uneven and overgrown climb sucked the life from her legs, but adrenaline ran through her like rocket fuel and Vicky pushed on with everything she had, her lungs ready to burst, her head spinning, her mouth open wide to pull in the air that her blocked and swollen nose couldn't.

# Chapter Forty-Seven

No matter how wide Vicky stretched her mouth open, when she inhaled, she couldn't drag enough air into her tight lungs to satisfy her. Every step up the hill had drained her energy, and when she reached the top, she stopped. With her hands behind her head to open her chest up, she stood in the full force of the wind, gasped, and looked down at the community.

Unable to speak from her lack of breath, Vicky watched the activity below. It looked like the guards and Moira had appeared, but from her current position—and in the dark—she couldn't be sure ... until she saw how the woman walked. Prowling like a dominant lion, Moira didn't have her white fur coat on, but Vicky recognised her from the way she stalked the courtyard and stopped outside Vicky's empty cell. A second later she moved over to the larger cell with all the prisoners in it. Vicky's heart beat harder than ever as she watched.

"Where's she gone?" the deranged woman yelled, her shrill call an unhinged and broken cry that shot out into the night. "Where's she gone?"

The other prisoners recoiled from her wrath and they all

gathered into one corner of the cell. "They're not telling her," Vicky said between breaths. "I thought someone would rat me out."

Flynn said nothing as he watched events unfold below.

"Did you see what she did to that girl?" Vicky asked him.

"The one they put in the hole?"

A shiver snapped through Vicky. "To think of the poor cow down there as we speak, surrounded by the rotting heads of the diseased in what sounded like a tiny dark space."

"You!" Moira called out and pointed into the cage of prisoners.

A man withdrew from her accusatory finger and his fellow prisoners stepped away from him. Three guards armed with bats and long blades entered the cage. Two of them grabbed an arm of the man each while the third pointed a machete at him.

The man shook and twisted as if to writhe free of the guards' grasp. But he clearly didn't have the strength for an escape. Broken by fear and weaponless, he fell limp and let the guards lead him from the cell.

Once they'd left the cage, the guards shoved him forward and he fell to his knees in the courtyard. Moira walked toward him with a long, curved blade in her hand. She pressed it to the man's neck, and still the man said nothing.

"Do you think he doesn't know where you've gone?" Flynn said.

"I don't know. Maybe he's ready to go himself. Maybe he'd rather die than give Moira what she wants. Withholding information is the only power they have over her now."

Without even questioning the man, Moira ripped her blade across his throat. Frozen with shock, the only sound Vicky heard came when his limp body hit the cold concrete.

Despite the distance between them and the dark, Vicky saw blood drip from Moira's blade as she pointed it at the next prisoner. Before the guards could go to the woman singled out by the vicious community leader, Vicky put her fingers into her mouth and whistled so hard it rang through the night.

As one, Moira and the guards turned to look up at her.

Again, despite the distance and the dark, Vicky felt Moira's glare bore into her and she stared back. When one of the guards stepped forward as if to run up the hill, Moira held a restraining arm across his chest and shook her head. They wouldn't catch Vicky and she knew it.

For at least two minutes, Vicky and Moira stared at one another before the vicious older woman pointed at the gate. Two guards ran over and locked it with a fresh padlock. Moira then walked back toward the buildings behind the cages. The woman seemed to know when she'd been beaten, but anxiety turned over in Vicky's gut as she watched her walk away. They'd not seen the last of each other. Not by a long shot.

# Chapter Forty-Eight

With their backs to Moira's community, Vicky and Flynn walked toward Home. It might have been dark and they might have had to remain vigilant for the diseased, but Vicky allowed herself a deep breath of freedom. The fresh air cleared out the lingering memory of the smell of human excrement, and she lifted her chest, empowered by her release.

"So how did you know where I was?" Vicky asked.

"When you left with Hugh, I followed you," Flynn replied. "I persuaded the kid on the door to keep quiet about letting me out. I told him to lock the door behind me and not to worry about me getting back in. After what you'd said about Hugh, I was worried something like this would happen."

"And Hugh didn't see you leave?"

"No. I had to let them take you into that community while I waited for Hugh to go back to Home though. Sorry."

Although Vicky continued to walk, she pulled Flynn close to her with a one-armed hug. "Don't be sorry. You came and got me. Thank you. Thank you so much."

When Flynn looked up at her, a deep frown creased his brow.

"What's up?" Vicky asked.

"Your eyes. I've never seen you with black eyes before. I dunno, it hurts to see you like this."

"You're a kind young man, Flynn. Thank you."

\*\*\*

They arrived at the end of the solar panel field. Vicky and Flynn crouched down in the long grass. As always, the wind ran over the environment, unimpeded because of the lack of tall buildings in the area and not many trees.

"And you think Hugh told you the truth about this way into Home?" Flynn said.

Three hundred and twenty-seven solar panels sat spread out before them. "They stretch back so far, it would make sense that these ones at the end are out of the reach of the cameras. So yeah, I do think he told me the truth."

A shrug and Flynn focused on the shiny black panels in front of them. "Only one way to find out, I suppose."

As Flynn moved forward at a crouch, Vicky nearly dragged him back. She had an instinct to go first like she always had, but she checked herself. Flynn had proven more than capable outside Home. She had to let him grow up. Fighting her maternal instinct, Vicky held back as Flynn crawled beneath the panel closest to them.

The grass around the solar panels had been stamped down, but the grass beneath them had been left to grow free. The long green blades stretched from the ground and pushed up beneath the bottom of the panels.

Vicky had her eyes closed for half of their journey as the grass brushed against her face. Every once in a while, one of the blades would threaten to cut her when she felt the sharp edge of it against her skin.

The panels had been placed so close together, Vicky and Flynn only exposed themselves for a second as they darted from the safety of one panel to the cover of the next. If they hadn't been spotted entering the field, it would take a keen eye to see them as they made their way through it.

Moving at a crouch set fire to the muscles in Vicky's tired legs, and she grimaced with every step, but she pushed on and kept moving forward on the tail of the younger and fitter Flynn.

\*\*\*

By the time they'd reached the end of the solar panel field closest to Home, Vicky's body screamed in agony and sweat stung her eyes from where it ran into them.

The camera that overlooked their approach sat on a pole close to the last panel. A quick glance up and Vicky saw it pointed out over the field. No way would it see them in their current position.

This time, Vicky took the lead as she slipped from beneath the final panel into the space behind the camera on the tall pole. Directly above the door to home, they stood in the middle of a ring of cameras, all of the glass eyes pointing outwards.

With Flynn by her side, Vicky walked to the edge of the small hill that the front door of Home nestled in. She peered down at it. Sooner or later Hugh would come out of that door. And when he did, they'd be ready for him.

# Chapter Forty-Nine

The sun warmed Vicky's face as she and Flynn sat on the grass bank above the front door to Home and waited. Tiredness stung her eyes from where she'd stayed awake all night, and her body ached, but she had to be ready for him. Hugh would leave Home at some point. He left most days, if for no other reason than to check the solar panels.

When the snap of the bolts on Home's front door issued their loud report, Vicky and Flynn looked at one another and shifted as close to the edge as they could without falling down.

"You don't have to do this," a small voice called out. "Please, you don't have to do this."

A woman that Vicky recognised from the community appeared beneath them, her hands bound together with cable ties.

"Actually," Hugh said, "I do. You do nothing for this community other than drag it down. We can't carry freeloaders like you anymore. I said you should go to the gym at least, but you couldn't even get your fat arse down there, could you?"

"I have bad knees."

"Tell that to the diseased, they may give you a head start."

The woman cried harder than before and walked back toward Home as if trying to force her way past him, but Hugh pushed her out again.

When she fought against him, Hugh's face twisted into a mask of hate and he grabbed a hold of her throat. With clenched teeth, he squeezed and forced the woman back out again.

Without a second thought, Vicky jumped down so she landed between Hugh and his way back in. Shock spread his features wide, and before he could react, Vicky had punched him three times in the centre of his face.

Hugh reeled, but he didn't have time to recover before Flynn jumped down and punched him too. Both of them rained a flurry of blows into the man until he fell. While he lay on the ground, Vicky kicked him so many times it hurt her foot.

It took Flynn pulling her back for Vicky to realise she'd knocked Hugh out cold. Out of breath and with sweat running down her face, Vicky looked at the woman with the cable-tied hands. A mix of fear and relief twisted through the woman's features in equal measure, and she said, "Thank you." Although it sounded more like a question than an expression of her gratitude. Should she be thanking this crazy woman and boy?

"Hugh kicked me out because I found out he'd murdered Jessica," Vicky explained. "Were it not for Flynn following me, I wouldn't have ever made it back." A glance at Flynn and Vicky saw his flushed cheeks before she turned back to the woman. "Flynn and I haven't been here long, so we're going to need your help to convince the community that Hugh's bad for them. Food's running low, which is why he's kicking people out. The people need to know about the food situation and what he did to Jessica. If they know, then at least we can do something about it as a group."

The woman had watched Vicky with her mouth agape.

When Vicky finished, she asked the woman, "Are you ready to help us?"

After a gulp, the woman nodded and the three of them re-entered Home, dragging the unconscious Hugh with them.

# Chapter Fifty

After she'd slipped the second lock on the front door into place, Vicky turned around and jumped to see Serj standing at the top of the stairs that led down into the canteen. They'd been clear only a second earlier. With a raised eyebrow, he looked from Vicky to the unconscious Hugh to Flynn and back to Vicky. "Uh … what the fuck?" He ignored the woman they had with them.

Flynn had the good sense to step forward. Closer to Serj than Vicky, it would sound better coming from him. "Among other things," he said, "Hugh was having sex with Jessica."

The words seemed to drag the air from Serj's body and he leaned forward a little, his mouth agape.

"I'm sorry to tell you this way, Serj, but we need you to trust us and not Hugh. He's a rat. Help us lock him up and we'll prove it to you."

Clearly still reeling from the bombshell he'd just had dropped on him, Serj stared at Flynn, a glaze of tears spreading across his eyes. After several gulps, he nodded. "If I'm honest, I knew something was up." Vicky watched the man break in front of her. He shook his head and slumped as if defeated. "I suppose I didn't want to admit it. What else could I do? Leave her? Leave Home?" Serj looked down at the unconscious Hugh through narrowed eyes. "So we need to lock him up?"

Vicky and Flynn nodded in unison.

"And then what?"

Vicky stepped forward this time. "Then we put him on trial. The community need to see what he's done."

The woman who Hugh had tried to evict—Sally—stepped aside and handed Serj the unconscious man's right arm. He grabbed it, stared down at the knocked-out Hugh and then nodded at the canteen. "People will ask questions when they see him like this," Serj said. "There's no way we can drag him through this place unnoticed."

"Tell them to come to the canteen in one hour and we'll explain everything," Vicky said.

After another pause, Serj looked back at Vicky. "I'm trusting you here. Don't let me down."

\*\*\*

In the hour between locking Hugh up and starting the case against him, Vicky had gathered all of the evidence she could find. Hugh had clearly been too confident in his leadership role at Home. Someone with a little more paranoia might have hidden a few things, but Hugh had made Vicky's job incredibly easy.

Vicky now stood in the canteen in front of everyone in Home like she had a few days previously. Every face in the cabbage-scented room seemed to focus on Vicky, the collective attention burning her like the sun. But Vicky said nothing as she waited and gulped an arid mouthful of hot air.

A few seconds later, Serj and Flynn led Hugh into the room, his hands cable tied behind his back.

Although he'd been silent as he walked in, when Hugh looked at the people of Home, he twisted and writhed against his restraint. "This is ridiculous. Let me the fuck go. Who do you think you are?"

But no one answered. Instead, Flynn and Serj led Hugh to the same seats at the front that they'd put the convicted men in a few days prior.

To spend some of the anxious energy that ran through her, Vicky paced up and down. The second Hugh's bottom hit the seat they'd reserved for him, she started, her words coming out fast, fuelled by the adrenaline of her nerves.

"You're standing trial for the murder of Jessica and many others."

The crowd gasped and Hugh shouted over the top of them, "What?"

"We believe you to be a danger to Home, and we plan on letting the people here decide whether we should kick you out or not."

Although Hugh shook his head, he didn't reply. Instead, he stared hate at Vicky.

"Ladies and gentlemen," Vicky said as she addressed the crowd of people. A slight shake took control of her voice and her lungs tightened as if shrinking. She cleared her throat and continued. "I put to you that Hugh is a danger to this community. Not only is he a danger, but he's a murderer, a cheat, *and* a liar."

Although Hugh scoffed, he didn't reply.

"Let me start first with his military background."

"What's that got to do with anything?" Hugh said.

"Nothing," Vicky replied, "because you don't have one. 'Door-kicking in Mogadishu'? What the hell, Hugh? I think you've read one too many space marine novels."

With his lips pinched so tightly his mouth ran as a horizontal line on his face, Hugh glared at Vicky.

"Good," Vicky said. "You don't deny that was a lie."

And he didn't. Maybe he knew he'd have to defend some far more controversial accusations and he'd chosen to pick his battles.

Vicky walked close to the crowd and pointed at her two black eyes. "I got these from a community no more than a fifteen-minute walk from here. Many of you haven't been outside of Home, but Hugh has allowed this community to exist, despite knowing the depths of their evil." Surprisingly, Hugh remained quiet as Vicky relayed the details of Moira's community and what they did to people. When she finished by explaining that Hugh had sent her down there on purpose, many of the gathered crowd tutted, shook their heads, and threw dirty looks Hugh's way.

"While I was caged in Moira's community, I saw a man who worked in the farm here. Hugh locked him up—or at least that's what he said he did—it turns out he actually kicked him out because the man had started to cause trouble. But I found out that he was causing trouble because he knew our food was running out and he wanted to do something about it. Isn't that true, Piotr?"

The large farmer looked up, his face flushed from the attention that suddenly turned his way. After he'd looked around the room, he turned back to Vicky and nodded.

"And that's why I've made people go to the gym," Hugh said. "We need to train people up to go outside and help hunt and grow more food."

"So why did you tell me that the gym was too little, too late, Hugh?"

"I *didn't* say that."

"You told me that the people in Home were parasites and the place should be purged of anyone who couldn't make themselves useful. You told me that Jessica found out about your plans to evict lots of people and challenged you about it. She also wanted to call off the affair she was having with you, right?"

Red-faced and tight-lipped, Hugh ground his jaw at Vicky as more gasps came from the crowd.

After a quick glance at the clearly distressed Serj, Vicky returned her attention to the crowd. "I've found several pieces of evidence in Hugh's room that link him to the crimes I'm accusing him of." She produced the first one and held it up for the crowd to see. "For those of you at the back, this list has everyone's name on it. Next to each name is a number between one and ten. Now, although the key isn't here for what each number means, I have a good hunch that it's about how useful Hugh thinks each person is."

Although Hugh tried to speak, Vicky spoke over him as she pointed at one of the names. "Sally Jacks," she said. "Can you please stand up, Sally?"

The woman got to her feet.

"Thank you. Where did we find you this morning, Sally?"

A shake ran through the woman and she cleared her throat before she replied, "Hugh was kicking me out."

"Thank you, Sally." Once the woman had sat down, Vicky turned back to the crowd. "So maybe it's a coincidence that Sally's a two on this list, but maybe it's not. And by the way, she's not the only two."

"This is all speculation," Hugh said. "You don't have the first clue what you're talking about. You …"

Hugh lost his words when he saw Vicky pull out a letter. He knew exactly what letter she had, and he knew what it meant.

"This is a letter from Jessica," Vicky said, the stillness so complete in the room it almost choked her. "Let me read you an excerpt." Vicky cleared her throat. "You need to rethink your plans. You can't kill everyone you deem to be useless. I know you call it setting them free, but you and I both know they won't survive, especially with their hands tied together. I implore you not to go ahead with this."

When Vicky looked up from the letter, she glanced first at the crowd. Many open mouths stared back at her. A look at Hugh and she saw him drop his head and stare at the floor. Any fight he might have had had just been ripped from him.

With no sense of satisfaction, Vicky turned to the crowd. "So I think it's pretty clear what Hugh was planning to do. And I, for one, think we should evict him before he can kill anyone else. Who here's with me?"

# Chapter Fifty-One

If someone had asked Vicky to guess how Hugh would react to his eviction from Home, based on his previous reaction to the diseased in the abandoned office building, she would have had him down as a snivelling wreck.

Not so.

Instead, Hugh stared at her, hatred continuing to burn in the polished oak of his irises. The man that currently stood in front of her had accepted his fate, but he did so with a silent promise to wait for her in the afterlife.

Everyone had followed Vicky, Serj, and Flynn up from the canteen with their bound prisoner. The case they'd put against Hugh had been enough to inspire hatred in the mob and a thirst for retribution, not only for Jessica, but for what he'd planned to do to most of them too.

"Normally," Vicky said and the crowd fell silent, "I'd ask you if you had any last words. But I don't think anyone has any interest in hearing them."

The sides of Hugh's wide jaw swelled and settled down again at the clenching and relaxing of his bite. Violence clearly coiled within the man, but it had no release; his wrists were bound tighter than he could wriggle out of.

A deep breath did little to settle the flip that turned through Vicky's stomach at what she had to do. Everything seemed to move in slow motion as she stepped toward the door and undid the first of the two bolts.

The *crack* rang out like a gunshot inside her skull. Her head spun when she leaned down and released the second lock with another *crack*.

When she stood up, Flynn put his hand in the centre of her back and raised his eyebrows at her. Vicky nodded that she was okay, drew one final breath, and pulled the door wide.

As Serj and Flynn led him from the foyer, Hugh watched Vicky and Vicky watched him back. A thousand words hurtled between the two, but neither spoke.

Once he'd passed her, Hugh didn't look around again. Instead, he stared out at the tall grass and kept his head high, his wrists clamped together out in front of him.

After Serj and Flynn withdrew back into Home, Vicky closed the door and secured it with the two locks.

For a moment, silence surrounded Vicky again as she stared at the button for the alarm.

"Do you need me to press it?" Serj said.

A shake of her head and Vicky reached up. It should be her burden to carry. When she slapped the button with the palm of her hand, the pulsing alarm called out through the speakers that faced away from Home. A shrill and mechanical caw, it let the diseased know they had an offering for them.

Vicky moved to the window to the right of the door, and

when she looked through, Hugh had turned to face her. The sight made her jump and forced her back a step. A sheet of reinforced glass partitioned the metre that separated them. A ghost made from living flesh, Hugh continued to stare.

Where there would usually be noise from the crowd, they all stood mesmerised by Hugh's icy glare. They seemed as entranced by it as Vicky was.

A disturbance to the grass in the distance and Vicky saw the diseased appear. A pack of about seven or eight of the fuckers, they ran toward Home with all they had. Even over the alarm and through the thick windows, Vicky heard their furious screams. Still, Hugh fixed her with his rage. He must have heard his demise closing down on him, but he paid it no mind.

As the pack drew closer, tension wound so tight in Vicky she felt like she could snap.

When the first of the diseased crashed into the back of Hugh, it forced him forward so his face smashed into the window that separated him and Vicky. The entire room—Vicky included—jumped backwards as if they would break through the pane.

An explosion of blood stained the window where Hugh had collided with it. The pressure of the diseased behind him kept him upright as several more of them crashed into him. A second or two later they dragged him to the ground. Hugh's nose drew a line of blood down the glass as he went. All the while he watched Vicky and showed no sign of pain.

One of the diseased bit into the top of Hugh's shoulder. It kept its mouth locked on and blood spilled from the sides of its sealed bite. Hugh's khaki shirt turned dark with his blood.

Another diseased bit Hugh's face and tore a deep hole in his cheek. If it hurt Hugh, he didn't show it. Instead he remained fixed on Vicky.

In the moment before a person reanimated, they appeared to die. Even during that time, Hugh stared at Vicky, his glassy glare almost obsessive in how it locked onto her.

Vicky didn't need to see him get back up again. With a lump in her throat and her legs so weak she could barely walk, Vicky turned away from the window and stumbled back through the crowd toward the canteen.

# Chapter Fifty-Two

When Vicky walked into the canteen the next day, tired despite what must have been at least fourteen hours' sleep, she looked at all of the people gathered there. Most of home seemed to be dotted around the room and she felt the eyes of every person in the place turn her way. Flynn sat at a table with Serj, so Vicky walked over to them and sat down.

Speaking from the side of her mouth, she said, "Am I being paranoid, or is everyone watching me?"

Both Serj and Flynn smiled.

"What's so funny?"

"We don't have a leader any more," Serj said. "I think the people may want you to do it."

"But I don't want it. I don't mind helping out, but I really don't want to run this place."

Flynn nudged Serj. "Why don't *you* do it?"

Serj shrugged like he wouldn't mind the position.

"Good," Vicky said. "It's settled, then."

"Someone needs to tell them," Serj replied. "And by someone, I mean you. Think of it as officially handing the baton over to me."

A deep sigh and Vicky stood up on her chair. On any other day, she might have needed to clear her throat to get their attention, or call out or even ring a bell. Today, however, every person in the room hung on her every action.

"We need a leader for Home now Hugh's gone."

Nods swirled around her and a few grunts of agreement.

"I know some of you think I would suit the task, but I'm really not leader material. I want to help run this place, but I can't be the main person here. I've just spoken to Serj and he seems up for the task."

A few shrugs, but most people nodded their acceptance of Serj as the new leader.

"Flynn and I will work closely by his side," Vicky said, "but Serj will have the ultimate say in what we do moving forward."

Before anyone had a chance to respond, Vicky sat down and Serj stood up in her place.

"We need to work out how to survive as a community," he said. "With food running out, we have to change and become more productive. We need to all contribute in the best way we can. And, from what Vicky's said, we have an unstable situation no more than fifteen minutes away from us. If we don't deal with the other community, we may end up regretting it. Besides, we have one of our own down there. I want this community to be just that: a community. When one of us is in need, all of us are in need. I'll be more than happy to hear suggestions from people as to how we'd be best taking our neighbours down, and if anyone has any other thoughts, then please let me know. But the way I see it, we need to get ready to fight."

Silence descended on the room. Piotr then stood up and

clapped his hands. The solitary sound called through the large area and up into the high ceiling. Another man from the farm stood up and joined in.

Soon, the swell of applause rushed through the room as each and every person in that canteen got to their feet and clapped Serj's speech.

In the almost deafening noise, Serj leaned down toward Vicky, the hint of a smile lifting his lips. "Maybe Hugh underestimated this lot."

As Vicky looked at the room, roused by Serj's speech, she smiled too and shook her head. "Maybe he did." She then turned to Flynn and raised her eyebrows. "It looks like we're going to war, mate."


Ends.

# Thank you for reading The Alpha Plague 5

The Alpha Plague 6 is avaialble now at
www.michaelrobertson.co.uk

Would you like to be notified when I have a new release?
Join my mailing list for all of my updates here:
www.michaelrobertson.co.uk

# Support the Author

Dear reader, as an independent author I don't have the resources of a huge publisher. If you like my work and would like to see more from me in the future, there are two things you can do to help: leaving a review, and a word-of-mouth referral.

Releasing a book takes many hours and hundreds of dollars. I love to write, and would love to continue to do so. All I ask is that you leave an Amazon review. It shows other readers that you've enjoyed the book and will encourage them to give it a try too. The review can be just one sentence, or as long as you like.

# Other Works Available by Michael Robertson

The Shadow Order - Available Now:

New Reality: Truth - Available now for FREE:

Crash - Available now for FREE:

Rat Run - Available Now:

For my other titles and mailing list - go to www.michaelrobertson.co.uk

# About The Author

Michael Robertson has been a writer for many years and has had poetry and short stories published, most notably with HarperCollins. He first discovered his desire to write as a skinny weed-smoking seventeen-year-old badman who thought he could spit bars over drum and bass. Fortunately, that venture never left his best mate's bedroom and only a few people had to endure his musical embarrassment. He hasn't so much as looked at a microphone since. What the experience taught him was that he liked to write. So that's what he did.

After sending poetry to countless publications and receiving MANY rejection letters, he uttered the words, "That's it, I give up." The very next day, his first acceptance letter arrived in the post. He saw it as a sign that he would find his way in the world as a writer.

Over a decade and a half later, he now has a young family to inspire him and has decided to follow his joy with every ounce of his being. With the support of his amazing partner, Amy, he's managed to find the time to take the first step of what promises to be an incredible journey. Love, hope, and the need to eat get him out of bed every morning to spend a precious few hours pursuing his purpose.

If you want to connect with Michael:

Subscribe to my newsletter at –
www.michaelrobertson.co.uk

Email me at –
subscribers@michaelrobertson.co.uk

Follow me on Facebook at –
www.facebook.com/MichaelRobertsonAuthor

Twitter at –
@MicRobertson

Google Plus at –
plus.google.com/u/0/113009673177382863155/posts

# OTHER AUTHORS UNDER THE SHIELD OF

### SIXTH CYCLE

**Nuclear war has destroyed human civilization.** Captain Jake Phillips wakes into a dangerous new world, where he finds the remaining fragments of the population living in a series of strongholds, connected across the country. Uneasy alliances have maintained their safety, but things are about to change. — Discovery **leads to danger.** — Skye Reed, a tracker from the Omega stronghold, uncovers a threat that could spell the end for their fragile society. With friends and enemies revealing truths about the past, she will need to decide who to trust. — **Sixth Cycle** is a gritty post-apocalyptic story of survival and adventure.

**Darren Wearmouth ~ Carl Sinclair**

### DEAD ISLAND: Operation Zulu

Ten years after the world was nearly brought to its knees by a zombie Armageddon, there is a race for the antidote! On a remote Caribbean island, surrounded by a horde of hungry living dead, a team of American and Australian commandos must rescue the Antidotes' scientist. Filled with zombies, guns, Russian bad guys, shady government types, serial killers and elevator muzak. Dead Island is an action packed blood soaked horror adventure.

**Allen Gamboa**

## *INVASION OF THE DEAD SERIES*

This is the first book in a series of nine, about an ordinary bunch of friends, and their plight to survive an apocalypse in Australia. — Deep beneath defense headquarters in the Australian Capital Territory, the last ranking Army chief and a brilliant scientist struggle with answers to the collapse of the world, and the aftermath of an unprecedented virus. Is it a natural mutation, or does the infection contain — more sinister roots? — One hundred and fifty miles away, five friends returning from a month-long camping trip slowly discover that death has swept through the country. What greets them in a gradual revelation is an enemy beyond compare. — Armed with dwindling ammunition, the friends must overcome their disagreements, utilize their individual skills, and face unimaginable horrors as they battle to reach their hometown…

Owen Baillie

## *WHISKEY TANGO FOXTROT*

**Alone in a foreign land.** The radio goes quiet while on convoy in Afghanistan, a lost patrol alone in the desert. With his unit and his home base destroyed, Staff Sergeant Brad Thompson suddenly finds himself isolated and in command of a small group of men trying to survive in the Afghan wasteland. **Every turn leads to danger**

The local population has been afflicted with an illness that turns them into rabid animals. They pursue him and his men at every corner and stop. Struggling to hold his team together and unite survivors, he must fight and evade his way to safety.

**A fast paced zombie war story like no other.**

W.J. Lundy

## *ZOMBIE RUSH*

New to the Hot Springs PD Lisa Reynolds was not all that welcomed by her coworkers especially those who were passed over for the position. It didn't matter, her thirty days probation ended on the same day of the Z-poc's arrival. Overnight the world goes from bad to worse as thousands die in the initial onslaught. National Guard and regular military unit deployed the day before to the north leaves the city in mayhem. All directions lead to death until one unlikely candidate steps forward with a plan. A plan that became an avalanche raging down the mountain culminating in the salvation or destruction of them all.

**Joseph Hansen**

## *THE GATHERING HORDE*

The most ambitious terrorist plot ever undertaken is about to be put into motion, releasing an unstoppable force against humanity. Ordinary people – A group of students celebrating the end of the semester, suburban and rural families – are about to themselves in the center of something that threatens the survival of the human species. As they battle the dead – and the living – it's going to take every bit of skill, knowledge and luck for them to survive in Zed's World.

**Rich Baker**

## *TOUR TO MIDGARD*

Tasked with a mission in Iraq, an Australian SAS patrol deploy deep behind enemy lines. But when they activate a time portal, the soldiers find themselves in 10th century Viking Denmark, a place far more dangerous and lawless than modern Iraq. The soldiers have no way back. Join the SAS patrol on this action adventure and journey into the depths of a hostile land, far from the support of the Allied front line. Step into another world…another time.

**Keith McArdle**

<<<<>>>>

Printed in Great Britain
by Amazon